QUEST

CITIES OF
GOLD AND GLORY

Written by
Dave Morris & Jamie Thomson

Illustrated by
Russ Nicholson

PRICE STERN SLOAN
Los Angeles

Published in 1997 by Price Stern Sloan, Inc.,
A member of The Putnam & Grosset Group, New York, New York.

0-8431-7927-9
First Edition
1 3 5 7 9 10 8 6 4 2

Cover illustration by Kevin Jenkins

Map illustration by Russ Nicholson

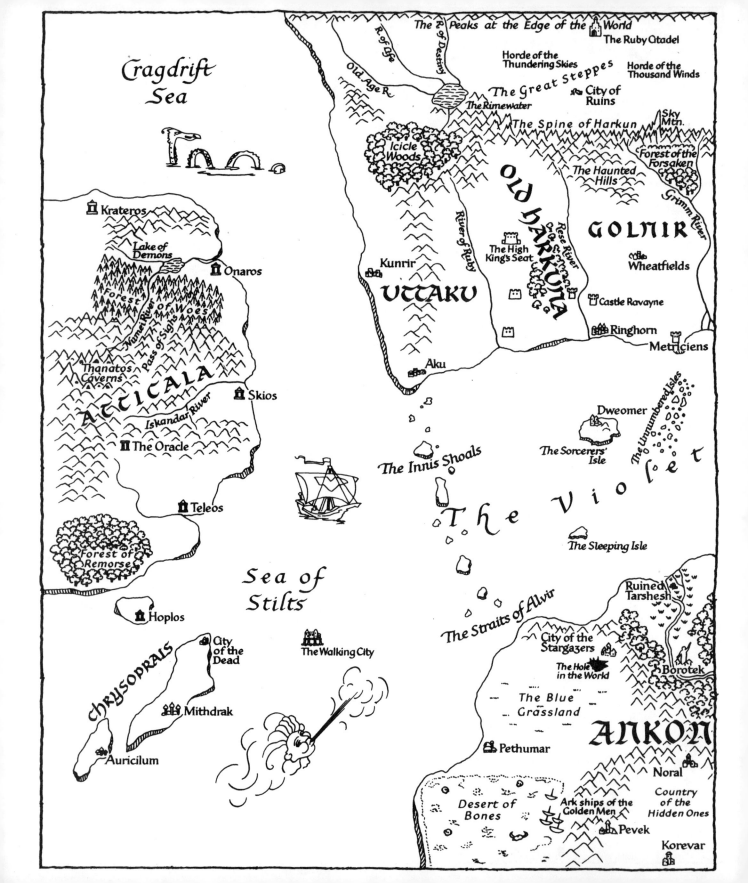

Cragdrift
Sea

The Peaks at the Edge of the World
The Ruby Citadel
Horde of the Thundering Skies
Horde of the Thousand Winds
The Great Steppes
City of Ruins
R. of Age
R. of Destiny
Old Age R.
The Rimewater
The Spine of Harkun
Sky Mtn.
Icicle Woods
OLD HARKUN
Forest of the Forsaken
The Haunted Hills
GOLNIR
Grimm River
Krateros
Lake of Demons
Onaros
River of Ruby
Rese River
Wheatfields
Kunrir
The High King's Seat
Forest
Numei River or Woes
Pass of Sighs
UTTAKU
Castle Ravayne
Thanatos Caverns
ATTICALA
Ringhorn
Metriciens
Skios
Iskandar River
Aku
The Oracle
The Unnumbered Isles
Dweomer
The Sorcerers' Isle
The Violet
Teleos
The Innis Shoals
Forest of Remorse
The Sleeping Isle
Sea of Stilts
Hoplos
The Straits of Alvir
Ruined Tarshesh
CHRYSOPRAIS
City of the Dead
The Walking City
City of the Stargazers
Borotek
The Hole in the World
Mithdrak
The Blue Grassland
ANKON
Auricilum
Pethumar
Noral
Desert of Bones
Country of the Hidden Ones
Ark ships of the Golden Men
Pevek
Korevar

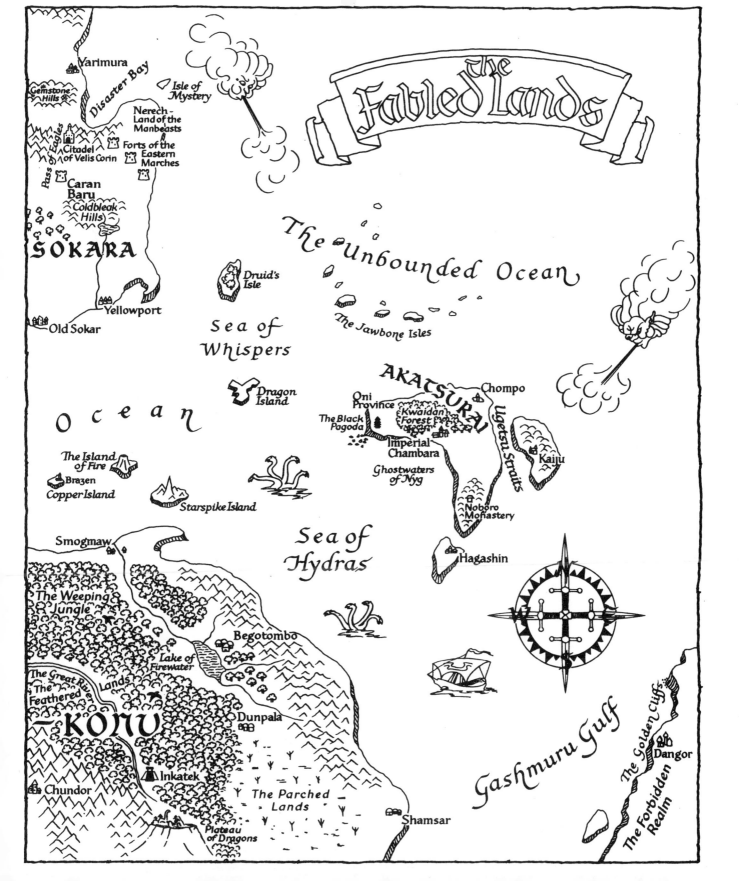

Starting characters

You can create your own character, or pick one from the following—except for the last two listed. Transfer the details of the character you have chosen to the Adventure Sheet.

LIANA THE SWIFT

Rank: 2nd
Profession: Wayfarer
Stamina: 13
Defense: 8
Money: 16 Shards

CHARISMA: 2
COMBAT: 5
MAGIC: 2
SANCTITY: 3
SCOUTING: 6
THIEVERY: 4

Possessions: **spear, leather jerkin (Defense +1), map**

Liana prefers to make her home in mountain grottos and woodland groves rather than in the squalid streets of cities. She has the agility of a gazelle, the cunning of a fox and the ferocity of an eagle. Despite her wild streak, she has a knack of making friends, for people sense that she is honest and trustworthy.

ANDRIEL THE HAMMER

Rank: 2nd
Profession: Warrior
Stamina: 13
Defense: 9
Money: 16 Shards

CHARISMA: 3
COMBAT: 6
MAGIC: 2
SANCTITY: 4
SCOUTING: 3
THIEVERY: 2

Possessions: **battle-axe, leather jerkin (Defense +1), map**

Andriel seeks fame through adventure and the glory of battle. He left his homeland when an extended outbreak of peace made his skills redundant there. He is blunt and outspoken, but scrupulously follows the warrior's code. If someone crosses him, he will use all the means at his disposal to get revenge.

CHALOR THE EXILED ONE

Rank: 2nd
Profession: Mage
Stamina: 13
Defense: 5
Money: 16 Shards

CHARISMA: 2
COMBAT: 2
MAGIC: 6
SANCTITY: 1
SCOUTING: 5
THIEVERY: 3

Possessions: **staff, leather jerkin (Defense +1), map**

Chalor is an outcast by choice, shunning his native land and the family who spurned him, driven by a burning desire for secret knowledge. His goal is to become one of the mightiest wizards of the world, and he is determined that nothing will stand in his way.

MARANA FIREHEART

Rank: 2nd
Profession: Rogue
Stamina: 13
Defense: 7
Money: 16 Shards

CHARISMA: 5
COMBAT: 4
MAGIC: 4
SANCTITY: 1
SCOUTING: 2
THIEVERY: 6

Possessions: **sword, leather jerkin (Defense +1), map**

Marana is a fiercely independent woman who grew up in the backstreets of her home town. Forced to flee because she was too active in her chosen profession, she has come to new lands to seek her fortune. Devious, resourceful, personable and intelligent, she can break in almost anywhere—and talk her way out afterwards! She is determined to get rich any way she can.

IGNATIUS THE DEVOUT

Rank: 2nd
Profession: Priest
Stamina: 13
Defense: 5
Money: 16 Shards

CHARISMA: 4
COMBAT: 2
MAGIC: 3
SANCTITY: 6
SCOUTING: 4
THIEVERY: 2

Possessions: **mace, leather jerkin (Defense +1), map**

Ignatius is a traveler whose desire is to learn all he can about the deities of these Fabled Lands. His strong beliefs give his sermons added zest, and he has enthralled many a crowd with his impassioned speeches. He has sworn to stamp out impiety wherever he finds it.

ASTARIEL SKYSONG

Rank: 2nd
Profession: Troubadour
Stamina: 13
Defense: 6
Money: 16 Shards

CHARISMA: 6
COMBAT: 3
MAGIC: 4
SANCTITY: 3
SCOUTING: 2
THIEVERY: 4

Possessions: **sword, leather jerkin (Defense +1), map**

Astariel has the wanderlust, and chafes if he has to remain in one place for any length of time. He enjoys the freedom of the open road and the thought that he never knows what adventures each new day will bring. He lives by his wits and is a familiar figure at tavern firesides, where he regales travelers with his tales.

JAMIE THOMSON

Rank: 10th
Profession: Author
Stamina: 47
Defense: 20
Money: 3 Shards

CHARISMA: 6
COMBAT: 10
MAGIC: 8
SANCTITY: 6
SCOUTING: 1
THIEVERY: 9

Possessions: **Computer, containing total knowledge of the Fabled Lands of *Quest*.**

Jamie Thomson began in the role-playing business as assistant editor of *White Dwarf* magazine. His previous works include *Fighting Fantasy* gamebooks for Puffin, the *Way of the Tiger* series for Hodder, and a gamebook based on Channel 4's *Crystal Maze* series (with Dave Morris).

Quest is based on the fantasy world of Harkun he developed for a series of plays broadcast on Radio 5 in 1993 in the United Kingdom. His hobbies are cricket, role-playing, and computer games. He lives in Brixton, England.

DAVE MORRIS

Rank: 10th
Profession: Author
Stamina: 33
Defense: 14
Money: 203 Shards

CHARISMA: 6
COMBAT: 4
MAGIC: 10
SANCTITY: 1
SCOUTING: 6
THIEVERY: 4

Possessions: **Maps revealing all of the Fabled Lands of *Quest*, including the underworld and places yet uncharted.**

Dave's interests include role-playing, Tibetan spirit dancing, films, boxing, travel, and food—especially food.

He is often to be found in the Chada restaurant in Battersea where he can be heard loudly expressing his views on most subjects under the sun.

He is married to one of the bacchantes.

Adventuring in the
Fabled Lands of QUEST

Quest is unlike any other gamebook series. The reason is that you can play the books in any order, coming back to earlier books whenever you wish. You need only one book to start, but by collecting other books in the series you can explore more of this rich fantasy world. Instead of just one single storyline, there are virtually unlimited adventures to be had in *Quest*. All you need is two dice, an eraser, and a pencil.

If you have already adventured using other books in the series, you will know your entry point into this book. Turn to that section now.

If this is your first *Quest* book, read the rest of the rules before starting at section 1. You will keep the same adventuring persona throughout the books—starting out as just a 2nd Rank wanderer in *Cities of Gold and Glory*, but gradually gaining in power, wealth, and experience throughout the series.

ABILITIES

You have six abilities. Your initial score in each ability ranges from 1 (low ability) to 6 (a high level of ability). The lowest possible score for an ability is 1—you can never have a lower score than that.

CHARISMA	the knack of befriending people
COMBAT	the skill of fighting
MAGIC	the art of casting spells
SANCTITY	the gift of divine power and wisdom
SCOUTING	the techniques of tracking and wilderness lore
THIEVERY	the talent for stealth and lockpicking

PROFESSIONS

Not all adventurers are good at everything. Everyone has some strengths and some weaknesses. Your choice of profession determines your initial scores in the six abilities.

Priest: CHARISMA 4, COMBAT 2, MAGIC 3, SANCTITY 6, SCOUTING 4, THIEVERY 2

Mage: CHARISMA 2, COMBAT 2, MAGIC 6, SANCTITY 1, SCOUTING 5, THIEVERY 3

Rogue: CHARISMA 5, COMBAT 4, MAGIC 4, SANCTITY 1, SCOUTING 2, THIEVERY 6

Troubadour: CHARISMA 6, COMBAT 3, MAGIC 4, SANCTITY 3, SCOUTING 2, THIEVERY 4

Warrior: CHARISMA 3, COMBAT 6, MAGIC 2, SANCTITY 4, SCOUTING 3, THIEVERY 2

Wayfarer: CHARISMA 2, COMBAT 5, MAGIC 2, SANCTITY 3, SCOUTING 6, THIEVERY 4

Fill in the Adventure Sheet with your choice of profession and the ability scores given for that profession.

STAMINA

Stamina is lost when you get hurt. Keep track of your Stamina score throughout your travels and adventures. You must guard against your Stamina score dropping to zero, because if it does you are dead.

Lost Stamina can be recovered by various means, but your Stamina cannot go above its initial score until you advance in Rank.

You start with 13 Stamina points. Record your Stamina in pencil on the Adventure Sheet.

RANK

You start at 2nd Rank, so note this on the Adventure Sheet now. By completing quests and overcoming enemies, you have the chance to go up in Rank.

You will be told during the course of your adventures when you are entitled to advance in Rank. Characters of higher

Rank are tougher, luckier, and generally better able to deal with trouble.

Rank	Title
1st	Outcast
2nd	Commoner
3rd	Guildmember
4th	Master/Mistress
5th	Gentleman/Lady
6th	Baron/Baroness
7th	Count/Countess
8th	Earl/Viscountess
9th	Marquis/Marchioness
10th	Duke/Duchess

POSSESSIONS

You can carry up to 12 possessions on your person. All characters begin with 16 Shards in cash and the following possessions, which you can record on the Adventure Sheet: **sword**, **leather jerkin (Defense +1)**, **map**.

Possessions are always marked in bold text, like this: **gold compass**. Anything marked in this way is an item which can be picked up and added to your list of possessions.

Remember that you are limited to carrying a total of 12 items, so if you get more than this you'll have to cross something off your Adventure Sheet or find somewhere to store extra items. You can carry unlimited sums of money.

DEFENSE

Your Defense score is equal to:

    your COMBAT score

    plus your Rank

    plus the bonus for the armor you're wearing (if any).

Every suit of armor you find will have a Defense bonus listed for it. The higher the bonus, the better the armor. You can carry several suits of armor if you wish—but because you can wear only one at a time, you only get the Defense bonus of the best armor you are carrying.

Write your Defense score on the Adventure Sheet now. To start with it is just your COMBAT score plus 3 (because you are 2nd Rank and have +1 armor). Remember to update it if you get better armor or increase in Rank or COMBAT ability.

FIGHTING

When fighting an enemy, roll two dice and add your COMBAT score. You need to roll higher than the enemy's Defense. The amount you roll above the enemy's Defense is the number of Stamina points he loses.

If the enemy is now down to zero Stamina then he is

defeated. Otherwise he will strike back at you, using the same procedure. If you survive, you then get a chance to attack again, and the battle goes on until one of you is victorious.

Example:

You are a 3rd Rank character with a COMBAT score of 4, and you have to fight a goblin (COMBAT 5, Defense 7, Stamina 6). The fight begins with your attack (you always get first blow unless told otherwise). Suppose you roll 8 on two dice. Adding your COMBAT gives a total of 12. This is 5 more than the goblin's Defense, so it loses 5 Stamina.

*The goblin still has 1 Stamina point left, so it gets to strike back. It rolls 6 on the dice which, added to its COMBAT of 5, gives a total attack score of 11. Suppose you have a **chain mail tabard (Defense +2)**. Your Defense is therefore 9 (=4+3+2), so you lose 2 Stamina and can then attack again.*

USING ABILITIES

Fighting is often not the easiest or safest way to tackle a situation. When you get a chance to use one of your other abilities, you will be told the Difficulty of the task. You roll two dice and add your score in the ability. To succeed in the task you must get higher than the Difficulty.

Example:

You are at the bottom of a cliff. You can use THIEVERY to climb it, and the climb is Difficulty 9. Suppose your THIEVERY score is 4. This means you must roll at least a 6 on the dice to make the climb.

CODEWORDS

There is a list of codewords at the back of the book. Sometimes you will be told you have acquired a codeword. When this happens, put a checkmark in the box next to that codeword. If you later lose the codeword, erase the checkmark.

The codewords are arranged alphabetically for each book in the series. In this book, for example, all codewords begin with B. This makes it easy to check if you picked up a codeword from a book you played previously. For instance, you might be asked if you have picked up a codeword in a book you have already adventured in. The letter of that codeword will tell you which book to check (i.e. if it begins with C, it is from Book 3: *Over the Blood-Dark Sea*).

SOME QUESTIONS ANSWERED

How long will my adventures last?

As long as you like! There are many plot strands to follow in *Quest*. Explore wherever you want. Gain wealth, power and prestige. Make friends and foes. Just think of it as real life in a fantasy world. When you need to stop playing, make a note of the entry you are at and later you can just resume at that point.

What happens if I'm killed?

If you have had the foresight to arrange a resurrection deal (you'll learn about them later), death might not be the end of your career. Otherwise, you can always start adventuring again with a new persona. If you do, you'll first have to erase all codewords, checkmarks and money recorded in the book.

What do the maps show?

The black and white map which precedes the rules shows the whole extent of the known Fabled Lands. The fold-out color map shows the land of Golnir which is covered by this book.

Are some regions of the world more dangerous than others?

Yes. Generally, the closer you are to civilization (the area of Sokara and Golnir covered in the first two books) the easier your adventures will be. Wait until you have reached higher Rank before exploring the wilder regions.

Where can I travel in the Fabled Lands?

Anywhere. If you journey to the edge of the map in this book, you will be guided to another book in the series. (*The War-Torn Kingdom* deals with Sokara, *Cities of Gold and Glory* deals with Golnir, *Over the Blood-Dark Sea* deals with the southern seas and so on.) For example, if you are enslaved by the Uttakin, you will be guided to *The Court of Hidden Faces* **321**, which refers to entry **321** in Book 5.

What if I don't have the next book?

Just turn back. When you do get that book, you can always return and venture onwards.

What should I do when traveling on from one book to the next?

It's very simple. Make a note of the entry you'll be turning to in the new book. Then copy all the information from your Adventure Sheet and Ship's Manifest into the new book. Lastly, erase the Adventure Sheet and Ship's Manifest data in the old book so they will be blank when you return there.

What about codewords?

Codewords record important events in your adventuring life. They "remember" the places you've been and the people you've met. Do NOT erase codewords when you are passing from one book to another.

Are there any limits on abilities?

Your abilities (COMBAT, etc) can increase up to a maximum of 12. They can never go lower than 1. If you are told to lose a point off an ability which is already at 1, it stays as it is.

Are there limits on Stamina?

There is no upper limit. Stamina increases each time you go up in Rank. Wounds will reduce your current Stamina, but not your potential (unwounded) score. If Stamina ever goes to zero, you are killed.

Does it matter what type of weapon I have?

When you buy a weapon in a market, you can choose what type of weapon it is (i.e. a sword, spear, etc). The type of weapon is up to you. Price is not affected by the weapon's type, but only by whether it has a COMBAT bonus or not.

Some items give ability bonuses. Are these cumulative?

No. If you already have a **set of lockpicks** (THIEVERY +1) and then acquire a **set of magic lockpicks** (THIEVERY +2), you don't get a +3 bonus, only +2. Count only the bonus given by your best item for each ability.

Why do I keep going back to entries I've already been to?

Many entries describe locations such as a city or castle, so whenever you go back there, you go to the paragraph that corresponds to that place.

How many blessings can I have?

As many as you can get, but never more than one of the same type. You can't have several COMBAT blessings, for instance, but you could have one COMBAT, one THIEVERY and one CHARISMA blessing.

1

The approach of dawn has turned the sky a milky gray-green, like jade. The sea is a luminous pane of silver. Holding the tiller of your sailing boat, you keep your gaze fixed on the glittering constellation known as the Spider, the sign under which you were born. It marks the north, and by keeping it to port you know you are still on course.

The sun appears in a trembling burst of red fire at the rim of the world. Slowly the chill of night gives way to brazen warmth.

You lick your parched lips. There is a little water sloshing in the bottom of the barrel by your feet, but not enough to see you through another day.

Sealed in a scroll case tucked into your jerkin is the parchment map your grandfather gave you on his deathbed. You remember his stirring tales of far sea voyages, of kingdoms beyond the western horizon, of sorcerous islands and ruined palaces filled with treasure. As a child you dreamed of nothing else but the magical quests that were in store if you too became an adventurer.

You never expected to die in an open boat before your adventures even began.

Securing the tiller, you unroll the map and study it again. You hardly need to. Every detail is etched into your memory by now. According to your reckoning, you should have reached the east coast of Harkuna days ago.

A pasty gray blob spatters on to the map. After a moment of stunned surprise, you look up and curse the seagull circling directly overhead. Then it strikes you—where there's a seagull, there may be land.

You leap to your feet and scan the horizon. Sure enough, a line of white cliffs lies a league to the north. Have you been sailing along the coast all this time without realizing the mainland was so close?

Steering toward the cliffs, you feel the boat judder against rough waves. A howling wind whips plumes of spindrift across the sea. Breakers pound the high cliffs. The tiller is yanked out of your hands. The little boat is spun around, out of control, and goes plunging in toward the coast.

You leap clear at the last second. There is the snap of timber, the roaring crescendo of the waves—and then silence as you go under. Striking out wildly, you try to stay clear of the razor-sharp rocks. For a while the undertow threatens to drag you down, then suddenly a wave catches you and flings you contemptuously up on to the beach.

You are battered, bedraggled, but alive. Now your adventures can begin. Turn to **559**.

2

Ringhorn receives goods from all along the Rese River, trading along the coast from Uttaku to Yellowport and south to distant Ankon-Konu. It is a very large, bustling city.

You can buy a town house here for 150 Shards. If you want to do that, cross off the money and put a checkmark in the box by the town house option.

Visit the market	turn to **232**
Visit the harbor	turn to **255**
Visit a tavern	turn to **311**
Visit your town house ☐ (if box marked)	turn to **278**
Visit the temple of Alvir and Valmir	turn to **301**
Visit the temple of Elnir	turn to **324**
Visit the temple of Sig	turn to **347**
Visit the merchants' guild	turn to **357**
Leave the city	turn to **370**

CITY OF RINGHORN

3

The merchants' guild in Wishport is too small to trade on behalf of its clients, but at least you can bank money here for safekeeping.

Make deposit or withdrawal	turn to **36**
Return to the town center	turn to **217**

4

The temple of Alvir and Valmir is a white marble building with a wide portico which gives a panoramic view of the harbor. The air in the nave is cool and fresh after the blazing sunshine outside.

Alvir and Valmir, the twin gods, are responsible for storms at sea. Sailors believe they take the souls of the drowned down to their halls beneath the vast deep.

Become an initiate	turn to **156**
Renounce worship of the twin gods	turn to **179**
Seek a blessing	turn to **202**
Leave the temple	turn to **217**

5

To gain admittance, you must make a CHARISMA roll against a Difficulty of 10.

Successful CHARISMA roll	turn to **28**
Failed CHARISMA roll	turn to **51**

6

The village of Delpton flourishes by the shipping of grain downriver to Ringhorn.

Visit the market	turn to **393**
Stop at an inn	turn to **418**
Leave Delpton	turn to **29**

7

The Forest of the Forsaken is a dark forbidding place. Even in broad daylight, shadows cluster like a mass of cobwebs under the gnarled boughs. As you skirt the forest searching for a path, you see a small village at the edge of the trees. A man looks up as you approach and starts to ring an iron bell.

Enter the hamlet	turn to **136**
Press on	turn to **159**

8

You see a hermit squatting beside a hut built of piled stones wadded with moss. Seeing you, he says: "Do you seek the key of stars? You'll find it at the end of a sinister path."

Go west on to the Whistling Heath	turn to **124**
Go east to the Monastery of Molhern	turn to **94**
Go south	turn to **54**
Go north	turn to **195**

9

Inside you find a set of steps winding down into the bedrock. At the bottom are three doors, each carved with a symbol. The symbol on the door to the left is a ram's head. The symbol on the central door is a fiery sun. The symbol on the right-hand door is a spider in a web.

Open the left-hand door	turn to **497**
Open the central door	turn to **522**
Open the right-hand door	turn to **547**
Leave the fort	turn to **373**

10

The shipyards of Metriciens are among the finest in the world, and no merchant wants to make do with a secondhand vessel to transport his precious wares. The best offers you can get are as follows:

Type	Sale price
Barque	190 Shards
Brigantine	380 Shards
Galleon	750 Shards

Remember to cross the ship off the Ship's Manifest if you go ahead with the sale. When you have finished your business here, turn to **33**.

11

You are on the road between Castle Ravayne and Wheatfields.

Head northeast to Wheatfields	turn to **120**
Head southwest to the castle	turn to **25**
Leave the road and go west	turn to **75**
Leave the road and go east	turn to **98**

12

Tekshin, the innkeeper, is a wingless mannekyn who dresses in a brocade vest and affects human mannerisms.

If you have the codeword *Bullseye*	turn to **487**
If not	turn to **610**

13

The blessing of Sig costs 10 Shards if you are an initiate, 30 Shards otherwise. If you buy the blessing, cross off the money and mark THIEVERY in the Blessings box on your Adventure Sheet.

The blessing works by allowing you to re-roll any failed THIEVERY attempt *once*. When you use the blessing, cross it off your Adventure Sheet. You can then make a second try at the roll.

You can have only one blessing for each ability at any one time. Once your THIEVERY blessing is used up, you can return to any branch of the temple of Sig to buy a new one.

When you are finished here, turn to **347**.

14

Your ship is sailing off the southeastern coast. "Wishport ahoy!" calls down the lookout.

Go west	turn to **175**
Go south	*Over the Blood-Dark Sea* **402**
Go east	*The War-Torn Kingdom* **222**
Dock at Wishport	turn to **325**

15

The nuns are instantly recognizable in their green and brown habits. Greeting you with friendly smiles, they offer to take you to the abbey.

Accept	turn to **61**
Refuse	turn to **312**

16

"The best buys in Metriciens are grain and cloth," a merchant advises you. Acquire the codeword *Bastion* if you didn't have it already.

Make an investment	turn to **85**
Check on investments	turn to **108**
Deposit or withdraw money	turn to **36**
Return to the town center	turn to **48**

17

You search the hydra's lair. Its treasure consists of 700 Shards, an **axe (COMBAT +1)**, a suit of **ring mail (Defense +2),** and a **candle**. Record anything you are taking on your Adventure Sheet, then turn to **640**.

18

You tell the high priest that you wish to renounce the worship of Nagil. He shows you your reflection in a mirror, then shatters it against the altar. When you ask if you must pay compensation to the temple, he shakes his head. "It is you who loses, not us."

Do you want to reconsider? If you are determined to renounce your faith, delete *Nagil* from the God box on your Adventure Sheet. You must lose any outstanding resurrection arrangements. Also lose the title *Chosen One of Nagil* if you have it. When you have finished here, turn to **257**.

19

The Three Fortunes are the goddesses of fate, who weave the tapestry of all men's lives. A placard outside the temple declares: *Join the temple and see your luck change overnight!* Inside, a vast wall painting shows a three-faced deity with six limbs hurling down nuggets of gold from a palace among the clouds.

Do you have the title *Beloved of the Three Fortunes*? If so,

turn to **180**. If not, turn to **203**.

20

"Get lost, you low-born dog," says a sentry, jabbing you with the butt of his halberd. Lose 1 point of Stamina and turn to **118**.

21

You find Estragon in his laboratory deep under the bedrock on which the castle rests. Crude stone steps wind down into a glimmering darkness filled with strange lights and fumes.

Estragon strides forward holding a vial of blue liquid which he is heating with incendiary spells. The glow of the chemicals throws his seamed old face into sharp relief against the backdrop of darkness.

Offer to run an errand for him	turn to **542**
You've completed an earlier errand	turn to **567**

22

You make your way along the woodland trail. At the point where three paths converge, an iron gallows hangs between two oaks.

Go south (toward the edge of the woods)	turn to **45**
Go west	turn to **367**
Go east	turn to **117**
Leave the path	turn to **380**

23

You are not sorry to be leaving the Forest of the Forsaken behind you. It is the most dangerous region of Golnir.

Head west	turn to **30**
Head east	turn to **99**
Head north	turn to **53**
Head south	turn to **122**

24

To renounce the worship of the Three Fortunes, you must pay 25 Shards to the priesthood by way of compensation. The priestess begs you to think again. "Those who worship the fateful trinity will surely prosper," she maintains. "But those who turn their back on the goddesses will soon meet them in their other guise—the dreadful weird sisters who preside at every man's deathbed."

Do you want to reconsider? If you are determined to renounce your faith, pay the 25 Shards and delete *The Three Fortunes* from the God box on your Adventure Sheet. When you have finished here, turn to **27**.

25

The white turrets of Castle Ravayne rise above the treetops.

CASTLE RAVAYNE

From the topmost tower flutters the black lion banner of the Ravayne clan. This is the stronghold of Vanna, Baroness of Ravayne.

Enter the castle	turn to **95**
Travel on further	turn to **118**

26

You are on the road that follows the banks of the Rese River between Castle Ravayne and the port city of Ringhorn. Roll two dice:

Score 2-5	Attacked by highwaymen	turn to **558**
Score 6-7	An uneventful journey	turn to **258**
Score 8-12	You meet a militia patrol	turn to **408**

27

The Three Fortunes are the goddesses of fate, who weave the tapestry of all men's lives. Their temple is a high-ceilinged edifice dimly illuminated by three altar candles.

Become an initiate of the Fortunes	turn to **225**
Renounce their worship	turn to **24**
Seek a blessing	turn to **271**
Leave the temple	turn to **217**

28

Here you can rest and recuperate if injured, join in the devotional rituals, or simply travel on to your next destination.

Recuperate from wounds	turn to **739**
Study at the monastery	turn to **763**
Pray to Molhern	turn to **780**
Talk to the abbot	turn to **126**
Travel on from here	turn to **74**

29

To travel on from here by river, you must pay a fare of 5 Shards. Otherwise you can cross the bridge and set out in the direction of the Singing Forest, or travel into the hinterlands.

Go west	*The Court of Hidden Faces* **111**
Take the road to Wheatfields	turn to **327**
Travel upriver	turn to **350**
Travel downriver	turn to **121**
Go north across open country	turn to **52**
Go south across open country	turn to **75**

30

You are in the broad valley of the Rainbow River. Close to the riverbanks, fertile soil means that there are many villages. Up on the wooded valley slopes, you see only the occasional stone-walled pasture. A peddler tells you that the countryside hereabouts has an eerie reputation.

Stay close to the river	turn to **303**
Venture further afield	turn to **326**

31

You are on the road that skirts the Whistling Heath and continues down toward the coast.

Head south toward Metriciens	turn to **193**
Go north to Wheatfields	turn to **71**
Leave the road and go west	turn to **98**
Leave the road to head east	turn to **195**

32

You are on the coastal road that snakes along the windswept clifftops between Ringhorn port and the market town of Metriciens. Roll two dice:

Score 2-5	Attacked by highwaymen	turn to **424**
Score 6-7	An uneventful journey	turn to **55**
Score 8-12	You·meet a militia patrol	turn to **449**

33

You are at the harborfront in Metriciens. Here you can buy a ship—or put one out to sea, if you have a ship docked at this location. It is also possible to visit the warehouses lining the waterfront, where goods from afar are bought and sold in quantity.

Buy a ship	turn to **331**
Sell a ship	turn to **10**
Go aboard your ship	turn to **164**
Hire crew for your ship	turn to **354**
Pay for passage on a ship	turn to **308**
Visit the warehouses	turn to **285**
Go to the city center	turn to **48**

34

An eerie glimmer shines between the trees that overhang the road a little way ahead. Venturing a little further, you see in the gathering darkness that an old iron gallows is set on one side of the road. The glowing light hangs around it like a bubble of marsh gas.

| Go closer to investigate | turn to **57** |
| Back off and wait till morning | turn to **11** |

35

You are on the road leading southeast from the market town of Wheatfields toward the Monastery of Molhern.

Head for the monastery	turn to **333**
Make for Wheatfields	turn to **71**
Head southwest toward the Whistling Heath	turn to **195**
Head north into the Endless Plains	turn to **328**

36

You can bank money with the merchants' guild by writing the sum you wish to leave with the guild in the box here. (Remember to cross it off your Adventure Sheet.) If you have banked any money with the guild in another book in the *Quest* series, add it now to this box and erase it from the other book.

To withdraw money from your account, simply transfer it

Money banked

from the box to your Adventure Sheet. The guild charges 10% on any withdrawals. (So if you withdrew 50 Shards, for example, they would deduct 5 Shards as their share. Round fractions in the guild's favor.)

When you are ready to leave:

In Ringhorn	turn to **2**
In Metriciens	turn to **48**
In Wishport	turn to **217**
In Wheatfields	turn to **71**
In Conflass	turn to **191**
If paying a ransom	turn to **229**

37

You are happy to share the fire on this cold night. As you sit on a pillow of dead leaves and watch the dancers, the heat of the fire makes you drowsy and your eyelids feel heavy because of the woodsmoke.

Make either a SANCTITY roll or a MAGIC roll (your choice) at a Difficulty of 15.

Successful SANCTITY roll	turn to **60**
Successful MAGIC roll	turn to **129**
Failed roll	turn to **83**

38

The time has come for you to take your leave of the Abbey of Lacuna.

Go north	turn to **7**
Go south	turn to **168**
Go east	turn to **99**
Go west	turn to **237**

39

Lose the codewords *Almanac, Brush,* and *Eldritch* if you have them.

You can invest money in multiples of 100 Shards. The guild will buy and sell commodities on your behalf using this money until you return to collect it. "Be advised that investments can go down in value as well as up," one of the guild traders reminds you.

Write the sum you are investing in the box here—or withdraw a sum invested previously. Once you're done, turn to **357**.

Money invested

40

Something about the man makes you suspicious. Pretending to need to answer a call of nature, you watch from a bush while he goes through your belongings. You bide your time until he is occupied before stealing back everything he took off you, plus a few of his own possessions for good measure. He suspects nothing, and when it is time for you to go your separate ways he bids you farewell with a cheery wave.

Going through the items you filched off him, you find a **lantern**, a **rabbit's foot charm,** and a **fishing hook**. Note these on your Adventure Sheet and turn to **349**.

41

Resurrection is free if you have the title *Chosen One of Nagil*. Otherwise it costs 200 Shards if you are an initiate, 600 Shards if not. It is the last word in insurance. Once you have arranged for resurrection you need not fear death, as you will be magically restored to life here at the temple.

To arrange resurrection, pay the fee and write *Temple of Nagil* (*Cities of Gold and Glory* **64**) in the Resurrection box on your Adventure Sheet. If you are later killed, turn to **64** in this book. You can only have one resurrection arranged at any one time. If you arrange another resurrection later at a different temple, the original one is canceled—cross it off your Adventure Sheet. (But you won't get a refund!)

When you are finished here, turn to **257**.

42

Becoming an initiate of the Three Fortunes gives you the benefit of paying less for blessings and other services the temple can offer. It costs 90 Shards to become an initiate. You cannot do this if you are already an initiate of another temple. If you choose to become an initiate, write *The Three Fortunes* in the God box on your Adventure Sheet—and remember to cross off the 90 Shards.

Once you have finished here, turn to **203**.

43

Tyrnai is the god of war. The idol in the shrine depicts him as a grim-faced warrior, jaws rimmed with blood, striding forth to do battle wielding an axe and a sword.

Become an initiate of Tyrnai	turn to **135**
Renounce his worship	turn to **158**
Arrange for resurrection	turn to **204**
Seek a blessing	turn to **181**
Leave	turn to **315**

44

Sir Debrumas, the steward, takes you in to the baroness's court. She sits in regal splendor on the gilded seat of House Ravayne. A banner showing the black lion crest hangs on the wall behind her. Although young and slender, she has the fierce unflinching gaze of one who is born to rule. "Why have you come?" she asks.

Undertake a quest	turn to **733**
Ask for a boon	turn to **709**
Assassinate the baroness	turn to **685**

45

A branch in the path to your left leads back out of the Forest of the Forsaken. The way ahead is overhung by low moss-sheathed boughs.

Leave the forest	turn to **23**
Carry on along the path	turn to **366**
Go back the way you came	turn to **22**

46

"When I was alive, I kept my treasure safe in a tower built of adamantine stone," the corpse tells you. "The tower had an impregnable door that could only be unlocked by a key made of star metal. But my death-sleep has been troubled by disquieting dreams. What if a living man should find the key and plunder my hoard?"

"And what is it you want of me?" you find yourself asking, your voice sounding hollow in the stillness of the crypt.

The corpse points past you, out to the south. "Go and find the key of stars. Bring it back to me. Then I shall permit you to take a reward." As you leave, you hear its parting words: "But take care not to return empty-handed, for then my vengeance would be swift and terrible."

Turn to **22**.

47

"Over here!" calls a plaintive voice from beyond a thicket. "Over here!"

Investigate	turn to **346**
Ignore the voice	turn to **93**

48

Metriciens is a large trading city of broad market plazas and great palaces built by the wealth of the merchant princes.

You can buy a town house here for 200 Shards. If you want to do that, cross off the money and put a checkmark in the box by the town house option.

Visit the market	turn to **194**
Visit the harbor	turn to **33**
Visit a tavern	turn to **778**
Visit your town house ❑ (if box marked)	turn to **171**
Visit the temple of Alvir and Valmir	turn to **148**
Visit the merchants' guild	turn to **16**

Visit the temple of Nagil	turn to **125**
Visit the temple of the Three Fortunes	turn to **102**
Leave the city	turn to **79**
Listen for rumors	turn to **56**

49

Lose the codewords *Almanac, Bastion,* and *Eldritch* if you have them.

You can invest money in multiples of 100 Shards. The guild will buy and sell commodities on your behalf using this money until you return to collect it. "Be advised that investments can go down in value as well as up," one of the guild traders reminds you.

Write the sum you are investing in the box here—or withdraw a sum invested previously. Once you're done, turn to **188**.

Money invested

50

"The best sailors are to be found in Metriciens and Ringhorn," an old sea-salt tells you. "But I might be able to muster a few boys to help out aboard your vessel."

It will costs 20 Shards to upgrade a poor crew to average. You cannot do any better than that here in Wishport. Once you've recorded any changes in the Ship's Manifest, turn to **325**.

51

You are rejected by the monks. "We cannot allow you to stay here," they say. "Your presence would disturb the atmosphere of serene contemplation."

It seems you must be on your way. Turn to **74**.

52

You are traveling across the fields and farmlands east of the Rese River. Roll two dice for encounters:

Score 2-6	An uneventful journey	turn to **212**
Score 7-12	A peddler	turn to **398**

53

Traversing the river valley down to the River Grimm, you reach a ford where you can cross to the east bank for 1 Shard. You could try swimming across, but the current is strong: you need to succeed at a SCOUTING roll at Difficulty 10 to do so.

Swim or pay to cross the river	*The War-Torn Kingdom* **123**
Failed attempt to swim	turn to **76**
Follow the riverbank south	turn to **99**
Strike out toward the forest	turn to **7**
Go north into the mountains	turn to **351**
Head west	turn to **372**

54

The country bordering the Whistling Heath is a place of undulating downs where blustery winds ruffle the treetops. Roll two dice:

Score 2-6	An execution	turn to **623**
Score 7	An uneventful journey	turn to **223**
Score 8-12	A small stranger	turn to **671**

55

You are on the coastal road. The great port city of Ringhorn is far to the west. The town of Metriciens is much closer.

Head west	turn to **373**
Head east	turn to **48**
Leave the road and head north	turn to **78**

56

There is naturally no shortage of rumors in a teeming city like Metriciens, where merchants come and go from all corners of the known world. Roll two dice:

Score 2-4	Honey for a thief	turn to **694**
Score 5-7	Political intrigue	turn to **718**
Score 8-9	Trade secrets	turn to **742**
Score 10-12	A bizarre tale	turn to **766**

57 ❑

If the box above is empty, put a checkmark in it now and turn to **80**. If the box is marked and you have a **flame opal eye**, turn to **103**. If the box is marked and you are not carrying the **flame opal eye**, turn to **11**.

58

You are on the road between Goldfall and the crossroads where Tekshin, the wingless mannekyn, has his tavern.

Head toward Goldfall	turn to **81**
Head toward Tekshin's Tavern	turn to **333**
Leave the road	turn to **123**

59

Amend your Adventure Sheet to show you are no longer an initiate of Sig.

You leave the temple and head off down a narrow street. After a few minutes, you think you hear a soft padding on the cobblestones behind. Are you being followed? Make a THIEVERY roll at a Difficulty of 13.

Successful THIEVERY roll	turn to **82**
Failed THIEVERY roll	turn to **105**

60

You wake up in the morning to find no sign that a camp was ever here. Perhaps you dreamed the whole thing. Rising, you set out on your way. Turn to **349**.

61

You are allowed to stay one night at the abbey. Recover 2 Stamina points if injured. "You must leave now," the nuns tell you at breakfast. "Only initiates may remain here among us."

If you wish to become an initiate of Lacuna you must convince the nuns of your sincerity by making a SANCTITY roll at Difficulty 12. (But you cannot try to become an initiate of Lacuna if you are already an initiate of another god.)

Become an initiate	turn to **84**
Leave	turn to **38**

62

To find out how well your investments have done, roll two dice. Add 1 to the dice roll if you are an initiate of the Three Fortunes. Also add 1 if you have the codeword *Brush*, add 2 if you have the codeword *Eldritch*, and add 3 if you have the codeword *Almanac*.

Score 2-4	Lose entire sum invested
Score 5-6	Loss of 50%
Score 7-8	Loss of 10%
Score 9-10	Investment remains unchanged
Score 11-12	Profit of 10%
Score 13-14	Profit of 50%
Score 15-16	Double initial investment

Now turn to **39**, where you can withdraw the sum written in the box there after adjusting it according to the result rolled.

63

Becoming an initiate of Elnir gives you the benefit of paying less for blessings and other services the temple can offer. It costs 60 Shards to become an initiate. You cannot do this if you are already an initiate of another temple.

If you choose to become an initiate, write *Elnir* in the God box on your Adventure Sheet—and remember to cross off the 60 Shards. Once you have finished here, turn to **2**.

64

You are restored to life at the Temple of Nagil in Wheatfields. Your Stamina is back to its normal score. The possessions and cash you were carrying at the time of your death are lost—cross them off your Adventure Sheet. Also remember to delete the entry in the Resurrection box now it has been used.

"Like fresh corn that grows after the burning of the stubble," declares the high priest, "so also are Nagil's followers restored to life eternal."

You leave the temple and drink deeply from a fountain in the town square. Turn to **71**.

65

To renounce the worship of the Three Fortunes, you must pay 30 Shards to the priesthood by way of compensation. The high priestess thinks you are being foolhardy. "How will you ever get rich if you turn your back on the threefold goddess?" she says.

Do you want to reconsider? If you are determined to renounce your faith, pay the 30 Shards and delete *The Three Fortunes* from the God box on your Adventure Sheet. When you have finished here, turn to **203**.

66

The armory in Castle Ravayne resounds with the ringing of hammers on anvils. The artisans here provide arms and armor for the greatest knights of Golnir. You can buy top-quality equipment, or sell anything you do not need:

Armor	To buy	To sell
Leather (Defense +1)	50 Shards	45 Shards
Ring mail (Defense +2)	100 Shards	90 Shards
Chain mail (Defense +3)	200 Shards	180 Shards
Splint armor (Defense +4)	400 Shards	360 Shards
Plate armor (Defense +5)	800 Shards	720 Shards
Heavy plate (Defense +6)	1600 Shards	1440 Shards

Weapons (sword, axe, etc)	To buy	To sell
Without COMBAT bonus	50 Shards	40 Shards
COMBAT bonus +1	250 Shards	200 Shards
COMBAT bonus +2	500 Shards	400 Shards
COMBAT bonus +3	1,000 Shards	800 Shards

When you have finished any business you want to do here in the armory, turn to **315**.

67

Becoming an initiate of Elnir gives you the benefit of paying less for blessings and other services that the temple can offer. It costs 60 Shards to become an initiate. You cannot do this if you are already an initiate of another temple.

If you choose to become an initiate, write *Elnir* in the God box on your Adventure Sheet—and remember to cross off the 60 Shards. Once you have done that, turn to **379**.

68

Here a knight has set up his pavilion. Encased from head to foot in plate armor, he sits astride his horse in silence while his dwarfish squire scurries forward on stunted legs to speak with

you. "My lord contests your right to use this path," the dwarf tells you. "You must fight him or else turn back."

If you have the codeword *Beltane*	turn to **251**
If not	turn to **274**

69

You step into a dark tower. As your eyes adjust to the gloom, you see a spiral staircase winding up and up. At the base of the staircase waits a huge slavering wolf. It would attack you at once if it were not attached to the wall by an iron chain.

Leave the tower	turn to **22**
Approach the wolf	turn to **161**

70

A wereboar in ornate armor comes thundering out of the undergrowth with a raised spear.

Wereboar, COMBAT 6, Defense 11, Stamina 8

There is no chance of retreat or surrender in this battle. If you win, turn to **323**.

71

Wheatfields is in the very heart of the fertile countryside of Golnir, and forms the hub of trade to the hinterland.

You can buy a town house here for 100 Shards. If you

WHEATFIELDS

decide to do that, cross off the money and put a checkmark in the box by the town house option.

Visit the market	turn to **165**
Visit the merchants' guild	turn to **188**
Visit your town house ❑ (if box marked)	turn to **211**
Visit the temple of Maka	turn to **234**
Visit the temple of Nagil	turn to **257**
Leave the town	turn to **286**

72

You spend a couple of months with the outlaws, during which time you have many opportunities to hone your questionable skills. Increase your THIEVERY score by 1. Your share of the loot amounts to 300 Shards.

At last you decide the time has come to move on; many other adventures await you. The outlaws are all hard men, but they have learned to look up to you. Several shed genuine tears to see you leave. Turn to **172**.

73

You get to talking to the captain of a small ship, who tells you that he will take you as far as Marlock City for 5 Shards. Another ship is sailing for Dweomer, and passage aboard that will cost 8 Shards. You can pay the fare and set sail, or stay in Wishport a while longer.

Set sail for Dweomer	turn to **261**
Set sail for Marlock City	turn to **266**
Don't put to sea yet	turn to **217**

74

Leaving the Monastery of Molhern behind, you travel on.

Take the road to Conflass	turn to **214**
Take the road to Metriciens	turn to **329**
Take the road to Wheatfields	turn to **352**
Head toward the Whistling Heath	turn to **8**

75

The region between Delpton and Castle Ravayne is a patchwork of tranquil fields and meadows. It seems that nothing intrudes on the slow contented pace of daily life hereabouts, but roll two dice for encounters in any case:

Score 2-4	Molhern's anvil	turn to **593**
Score 5-8	Uneventful journey	turn to **97**
Score 9-12	A rascal	turn to **423**

76

Lose 2-12 Stamina (roll two dice) as you are swept under. If you survive, turn to **689**.

77

You stand on the windswept Endless Plains and wonder where you should seek your next adventure.

Head north	turn to **259**
Head northeast to the Haunted Hills	turn to **305**
Search for the Tower of Despair	turn to **100**
Visit the town of Wheatfields	turn to **71**
Head toward the Rese River	turn to **52**
Go east	turn to **30**
Go south	turn to **123**

78

You head over the downs and strike out toward the hinterlands of Golnir. Roll two dice:

Score 2-5	An uneventful journey	turn to **222**
Score 6-7	Pipe music at night	turn to **728**
Score 8-12	Burial mounds at dusk	turn to **474**

79

From Metriciens, you have the option to put to sea or journey overland. To travel by sea, you must either possess a ship which is docked in the harbor here (check your Adventure Sheet) or find a sea captain who is willing to take you as his passenger.

Go to the harbor	turn to **33**
Take the coast road west	turn to **32**
Take the road to Wheatfields	turn to **147**
Take the road to Haggart's Corner	turn to **216**

80

You meet a pale figure loitering under the gallows. The hairs on the back of your neck rise when he steps forward and passes his hand right through you. "Yes, I am dead," he moans. "Wrongfully executed on this gallows for a crime I did not commit. The real murderer had me framed, but I'll be avenged on him yet, with your help. He wears a velvet patch over one eye. Find him and bring me what lies under the patch. I'll be grateful, never think I won't...."

He vanishes. A shiver passes up your spine. However long ago this crime was perpetrated, the spirit cannot have rest until his tormentor is dead.

Get the codeword *Bumble*, then turn to **11**.

81

Goldfall is a ramshackle town. The buildings are in poor repair, the livestock wanders untended in the fields. The reason is that most people who live here are just transients. They come from far and wide because of the stories that chunks of gold shower from the sky on certain nights. You pass a beggar squatting beside the town square and ask if he ever found any gold.

"Nope," he says. "But I heard of a guy that got rich from finding three nuggets each as big as your fist. Got any spare change?"

Visit the Temple of the Three Fortunes	turn to **19**
Lodge at an inn	turn to **695**
Search for gold	turn to **719**
Ready to leave	turn to **104**

82

You easily evade your pursuers. Crouching unseen in the shadows, you watch them blunder past. You smile to see them peering to and fro, frowning in annoyance at having lost you.

Perhaps you never really needed Sig's divine help. You seem to be just as lucky without it. Roll two dice. If the roll is higher than your current THIEVERY score, increase it by 1.

Once you've done that, turn to **2**.

83

You wake in the morning feeling chilled right through to the bone. You rise slowly, your limbs stiff and shaky. Perhaps you have a fever coming on?

Lose 1 point from your normal unwounded Stamina score. This loss is permanent. After making the alteration on your Adventure Sheet, turn to **349**.

84

You are accepted as an initiate of Lacuna, who is the moon goddess of the hunt. She protects travelers and madmen.

Seek a blessing	turn to **526**
Rest here a while	turn to **576**
Leave	turn to **38**

85

Lose the codewords *Almanac*, *Brush*, and *Catalyst* if you have them.

You can invest money in multiples of 100 Shards. The guild will buy and sell commodities on your behalf using this money until you return to collect it. "Be advised that investments can go down in value as well as up," one of the guild traders reminds you.

Write the sum you are investing in the box here—or withdraw a sum invested previously. Once you're done, turn to **16**.

Money invested

86

To renounce the worship of Elnir, you must pay 40 Shards to the priesthood by way of compensation. The high priest fixes you with a stern gaze. "Not everyone has the strength of character to make a good worshipper of Lord Elnir," he says, nodding. "Find yourself a less demanding deity."

Do you want to change your mind? If you are determined to renounce your faith, pay the 40 Shards and delete *Elnir* from the God box on your Adventure Sheet. When you have finished here, turn to **2**.

87

Becoming an initiate of Maka gives you the benefit of paying less for blessings and other services the temple can offer. It costs 30 Shards to become an initiate. You cannot do this if you are already an initiate of another temple.

If you choose to become an initiate, write *Maka* in the God box on your Adventure Sheet—and remember to cross off the 30 Shards. Once you have finished here, turn to **234**.

88

If you are an initiate it costs only 25 Shards to purchase The Three Fortunes' blessing. A non-initiate must pay 90 Shards.

Cross off the money and mark *Luck* in the Blessings box on your Adventure Sheet. The blessing works by allowing you to re-roll any dice result *once*. (This does not have to be an ability roll. You could also use it to re-roll an encounter result that you didn't want.) When you use the blessing, cross it off your Adventure Sheet.

You can only have one Luck blessing at any one time. Once it is used up, you can return to any branch of the temple of The Three Fortunes to buy a new one.

When you are finished here, turn to **203**.

89

You join the younger knights for some combat practice. These are friendly bouts, but the occasional injury is unavoidable. Roll one die; this is the number of Stamina points you lose.

Assuming you survive, you can now try to increase your COMBAT score. Roll a die and if you score higher than your COMBAT, add 1 to it.

When you have done all that, turn to **315**.

90

You must forfeit one weapon or suit of armor to the priests by way of compensation. If you are not carrying any armor or weapons, they will take any money you have on you instead. Cross off the item (or your money), delete *Elnir* from the God box on your Adventure Sheet, and then turn to **379**.

91

Cracks in the weathered masonry make it an easy climb. Soon you are within reach of the jeweled eye. It should be an easy matter to pry the emerald loose.

Attempt a MAGIC roll at a Difficulty of 12.

Successful MAGIC roll	turn to **114**
Failed MAGIC roll	turn to **137**

92

The sudden tolling of a great bell rings out from the top of the tower. Before you can move, you are seized by gaunt gray hands. Phantom figures have risen up out of the ground to surround you. "Your prying fingers have rung the bell to disturb our rest," whisper the figures. "Now we'll take you down with us to our abode."

To escape from them you must make a SANCTITY roll at a Difficulty of 13. This allows you to pass through their clutches and run off to the safety of the forest's edge.

Successful in SANCTITY roll	turn to **159**
Failed SANCTITY roll	turn to **115**

93

You are beginning to think you may be lost. Make a SCOUTING roll at a Difficulty of 10.

Successful SCOUTING roll	turn to **116**
Failed SCOUTING roll	turn to **139**

94

Molhern is the blacksmith of the gods, famous for his cleverness and the breadth of his knowledge. Here at the monastery, his most devout followers live an austere existence, striving to honor the god through a regimen of hard physical labor combined with academic study.

If you are injured, this is a good place to rest and recuperate from your wounds.

Stop off at the monastery	turn to **5**
Take the road to Conflass	turn to **214**
Take the road to Metriciens	turn to **329**
Take the road to Wheatfields	turn to **352**
Head toward the Whistling Heath	turn to **8**

95

If you are 4th Rank or higher, turn to **341**. If not, turn to **364**.

96

The warehouses in Wishport stock goods from many distant ports. The trick is to buy goods in an area where they are plentiful (and therefore cheap) and transport them to an area where they are in demand.

Prices are quoted here for entire Cargo Units. You cannot

THE MONASTERY OF MOLHERN

carry this large a quantity in person; you will need a ship to transport it.

Cargo	To buy	To sell
Furs	200 Shards	180 Shards
Grain	150 Shards	135 Shards
Metals	750 Shards	675 Shards
Minerals	700 Shards	630 Shards
Spices	900 Shards	810 Shards
Textiles	250 Shards	225 Shards
Timber	200 Shards	180 Shards

When you have completed your business, turn to **217**.

97

Traveling in the fertile valley of the Rese River.

Go north to Delpton	turn to **6**
Go south to Castle Ravayne	turn to **25**
Go east	turn to **120**

98

Here in the peaceful countryside of southwest Golnir, hay carts rumble down leafy lanes and peasants look up from their work with a cheery wave. The dangers that an adventurer must often face are easily forgotten in this idyllic setting. Roll two dice for encounters:

Score 2-6	A wise friar	turn to **448**
Score 7	Uneventful journey	turn to **235**
Score 8-12	A storyteller	turn to **473**

99

Lush cornfields are on one side, the surging river on the other. You reach a point where it is possible to ford the river across a causeway of ancient weathered stones.

Cross to east bank	*The War-Torn Kingdom*	**333**
Strike out to the west		turn to **122**
Go south		turn to **168**
Go north		turn to **53**

100

You seek high and low, but after many days you have to admit you are stumped. Even though there are many legends of the Tower of Despair in these parts, you cannot find any sign of it. Turn to **77**.

101

This part of the country is infamous as the haunt of brigands, smugglers, and witches. Roll two dice:

Score 2-6	Smugglers	turn to **360**
Score 7	Uneventful journey	turn to **268**
Score 8-9	Brigands attack	turn to **337**
Score 10-12	A coven meeting	turn to **499**

102

The temple of the Three Fortunes is a hushed, echoing hallway where a triple-branched candelabrum burns wanly on an altar of green stone. In the dim light you can make out a tapestry that depicts the three goddesses as a young maiden, a woman, and an old crone.

Become an initiate of the Fortunes	turn to **201**
Renounce their worship	turn to **224**
Seek a blessing	turn to **247**
Leave the temple	turn to **48**

103

The ghost comes as before. "You have returned with proof? Ah, the wretch's gemstone eye. Good, good!"

He takes the **flame opal eye** (cross it off) and seeps down into the dank soil. You dig and find a chest containing 250 Shards. Also gain 1 point of SANCTITY for having righted a wrong. Then turn to **11**.

104

You leave the covetous folk of Goldfall to wait for wealth to drop into their laps. You prefer to seek out your own fortune.

Take the road	turn to **332**
Strike off across open country	turn to **123**

105

As you turn into the small square beside the Founder's Fountain, a man wrapped in a gray cloak brushes swiftly past you. An instant later you realize he has stolen any money you had on you. (If you had no money, he stole one possession instead—you choose which.)

You whirl. There is no sign of the scoundrel. Make a SCOUTING roll at Difficulty 10 if you want to try to track him.

Successful SCOUTING roll	turn to **128**
Failed (or did not attempt) SCOUTING roll	turn to **151**

106

You are in the shallow coastal waters between Ringhorn and Metriciens. Roll two dice:

Score 2-4	Storm	turn to **607**
Score 5-7	Pirates	turn to **463**
Score 8-12	An uneventful journey	turn to **221**

107

To find out how your investments have done, roll two dice. Add 1 to the dice roll if you are an initiate of the Three Fortunes. Also add 1 if you have the codeword *Bastion*, add 2 if you have the codeword *Almanac*, and add 3 if you have the codeword *Eldritch*.

Score 2-4	Lose entire sum invested
Score 5-6	Loss of 50%
Score 7-8	Loss of 10%
Score 9-10	Investment remains unchanged
Score 11-12	Profit of 10%
Score 13-14	Profit of 50%
Score 15-16	Double initial investment

Now turn to **49**, where you can withdraw the sum written in the box there after adjusting it according to the result rolled.

108

To find out how your investments have done, roll two dice. Add 1 to the dice roll if you are an initiate of the Three Fortunes. Also add 1 if you have the codeword *Brush*, add 2 if you have the codeword *Almanac*, and add 4 if you have the codeword *Catalyst*.

Score 2-3	Lose entire sum invested
Score 4-5	Loss of 50%
Score 6-7	Loss of 25%
Score 8-9	Loss of 10%
Score 10-11	Investment remains unchanged
Score 12-13	Profit of 25%
Score 14-15	Profit of 75%
Score 16-17	Profit of 150%

Now turn to **85**, where you can withdraw the sum written in the box there after adjusting it according to the result rolled.

109

If you are an initiate it costs only 10 Shards to purchase Elnir's blessing. A non-initiate must pay 25 Shards.

Cross off the money and mark CHARISMA in the Blessings box on your Adventure Sheet. The blessing works by allowing you to try again when you make a failed CHARISMA roll. It is only good for *one* re-roll. When you use the blessing, cross it off your Adventure Sheet.

You can have only one CHARISMA blessing at any one time. Once it is used up, you can return to any branch of the temple of Elnir to buy a new one.

When you are finished here, turn to **2**.

110

To renounce the worship of Maka, you must pay 15 Shards to the priesthood by way of compensation. The high priestess explains that the cost of renouncing your initiate's vows may be more than financial. "Do you really want to lay yourself open to the goddess's displeasure?" she asks.

Do you want to change your mind? If you are determined to renounce your faith, pay the 15 Shards and delete *Maka* from the God box on your Adventure Sheet. When you have finished here, turn to **234**.

111

An inner room of the temple is given over to gambling games. You suspect this is where most of the locals' wealth ends up. You must pay 5 Shards to join in a game. At the far end of the room, a placard reads: *Sacred games—initiates only*.

Pay 5 Shards and gamble	turn to **134**
Join the sacred games (if an initiate)	turn to **157**

112

The doorway into the castle keep is guarded by elite knights in gleaming gem-studded armor. They watch you narrowly as you approach, then slowly cross their halberds to bar your path. "What is your business here?" asks one.

If you have the title *Paladin of Ravayne*, turn to **250**. If not, turn to **273**.

113

If you are an initiate it costs only 10 Shards to purchase Elnir's blessing. A non-initiate must pay 25 Shards.

Cross off the money and mark CHARISMA in the Blessings box on your Adventure Sheet. The blessing works by allowing you to try again when you make a failed CHARISMA roll. It is only good for *one* re-roll. When you use the blessing, cross it off your Adventure Sheet.

You can only have one CHARISMA blessing at any one time. Once it is used up, you can return to any branch of the temple of Elnir to buy a new one.

When you are finished here, turn to **379**.

114

A prickling of the hairs on the nape of your neck warns you that dire sorcery is at work here. The emerald is most probably cursed.

Take it anyway	turn to **137**
Descend and enter the crypt	turn to **160**
Go back and take the other path	turn to **22**
Leave the forest	turn to **23**

115

The ghosts tear you limb from limb and drag the severed portions down into the ground where they have their shallow graves. Unless you have arrangements for resurrection, this is the end.

116

You manage to get your bearings. A stream runs to the southeast and by following it you can reach the forest's edge.

Cross the stream	turn to **185**
Follow the stream	turn to **162**
Return to the path	turn to **22**

117

If you have the codeword *Bosky*, turn to **772**. If not, turn to **382**.

118

You can travel south toward the coast, or venture into the heartland of Golnir. Journeying by river costs 5 Shards.

Take the road north	turn to **304**
Take the road south	turn to **26**
Go east across open country	turn to **98**
Go west across the River Rese	*The Court of Hidden Faces* **222**
Follow the riverbank north	turn to **75**
Sail upriver	turn to **281**
Sail downriver	turn to **2**

119

Your ship is sailing in coastal waters close to Wishport. Roll two dice:

Score 2-4	Storm	turn to **509**
Score 5-6	Pirates	turn to **386**
Score 7-12	An uneventful voyage	turn to **14**

120

You come to an inn nestling against a fringe of trees beside a meadow full of flowers. The innkeeper, whose name is Chard, tells you that he does good business: "The merchants who travel between Wheatfields and Castle Ravayne are never short of money to spend."

Stop at the inn	turn to **143**
Take the road north	turn to **166**
Take the road south	turn to **304**
Head west cross-country	turn to **75**
Head east cross-country	turn to **98**

121

The strong current of the Rese River carries you swiftly south. Soon you see the battlements of Castle Ravayne in the distance. You can disembark at this point or journey on to the coast.

Visit Castle Ravayne	turn to **25**
Continue downriver to Ringhorn	turn to **2**

122

If you are an initiate of Lacuna then you have the option to visit the nearby abbey of your goddess. Non-initiates cannot usually find the path to the abbey, as it is hidden and protected by powerful spells, though you can attempt to uncover it by making a MAGIC roll at Difficulty 15 or a SCOUTING roll at Difficulty 18.

Initiate of Lacuna	turn to **336**
Find the path using MAGIC or SCOUTING	turn to **376**
Not searching for the abbey	turn to **359**

123

The farmers in these parts are ruddy-cheeked and jolly, always ready with a foaming mug of ale. If you took up every offer of hospitality, you would never reach your destination.

Roll two dice:

Score 2-6	Incident in a bull's field	turn to **741**
Score 7	Uneventful journey	turn to **199**
Score 8-12	A country fair	turn to **765**

124

The wind rips between high craggy peaks, producing the eerie wailing sound that gives the heath its name.

Go east	turn to **714**
Go west	turn to **642**
Go north	turn to **666**
Go south	turn to **690**

125

Nagil is the god of death, and is usually depicted as a cowled figure with a hollow black stare. Paradoxically, his temple is no

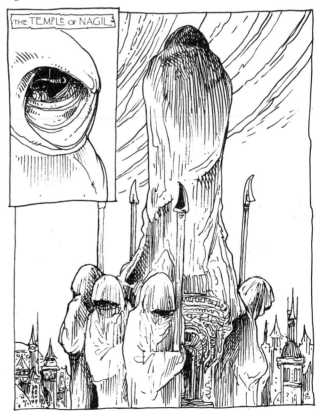

stately mausoleum, but a wide high-towered building from whose minarets a haunting melody is sung both at dawn and at dusk.

Become an initiate of Nagil	turn to **270**
Renounce his worship	turn to **293**
Make resurrection arrangements	turn to **316**
Leave the temple	turn to **48**

126

The abbot is pleased to tell you about the god Molhern. "Originally he was the god of craftsmen, blacksmiths, and stonemasons," he says.

"It was Molhern who gave mankind the secret of making fire. But he also taught the secret of writing, which is why he is the patron deity of scholars. Our library here is the most magnificent in the world."

If you have the codeword *Bumble*, turn to **149**. If not, turn to **28**.

127

You are on the road between Metriciens and Haggart's Corner.

Follow the road to Metriciens	turn to **48**
Follow the road to Haggart's Corner	turn to **150**
Head cross-country toward Wishport	turn to **101**
Head cross-country toward the heath	turn to **54**

128

The trail leads you down by the docks. Suddenly two men leap out at you from behind a pile of crates. They are brandishing deviltooth knives: sharp slivers of mottled yellow ivory that dissolve after use so that they leave no evidence.

Fight the two men one after the other.

1st Assassin, COMBAT 6, Defense 8, Stamina 7
2nd Assassin, COMBAT 7, Defense 8, Stamina 7
If you beat them, turn to **174**.

129

You've been around enough to know when you're in trouble. The dancers are more sinister than they seem. You pretend to fall asleep. The dancers become grinning skeletons prancing macabrely around the clearing. When they come closer to drink your blood, you leap up and drive them off with a protective rune.

Turn to **244**.

130

Here on the flat country of southeast Golnir, the River Grimm meanders before sluggishly debouching into the swampy delta of the Magwort Fens.

Go upriver to Conflass	turn to **168**
Go over the border into Sokara	*The War-Torn Kingdom* **99**
Go west	turn to **306**
Go south into the fens	turn to **219**

131

The merchants' guild in Conflass has close links with similar trade organizations across the border in Sokara. The guildmaster teaches you an old adage that he always applies when doing business: "For metals and minerals look to the east, but the grain you buy at home costs least."

Get the codeword *Brush*, then decide what you will do here:

Make an investment	turn to **154**
Check on investments	turn to **177**
Deposit or withdraw money	turn to **36**
Return to the town center	turn to **191**

132

Becoming an initiate of Alvir and Valmir gives you the benefit of paying less for blessings and other services the temple can offer. It costs 40 Shards to become an initiate. You cannot do this if you are already an initiate of another temple.

If you choose to become an initiate, write *Alvir and Valmir* in the God box on your Adventure Sheet—and cross off the 40 Shards. Once you have finished here, turn to **148**.

133

If you are an initiate it costs only 10 Shards to purchase Maka's blessing. A non-initiate must pay 20 Shards.

Cross off the money and mark *Immunity to Disease and Poison* in the Blessings box on your Adventure Sheet. The blessing works by allowing you to ignore any *one* occasion when you would normally suffer from disease or poison—for instance, the venomous bite of a snake. When you use the blessing, cross it off your Adventure Sheet.

You can only have one Immunity to Disease and Poison blessing at any one time. Once it is used up, you can return to any branch of the temple of Maka to buy a new one.

When you are finished here, turn to **234**.

134

You can gamble in multiples of 10 Shards. Decide how much you are wagering, then roll two dice:

Score 2-4	Lose your entire stake
Score 5-7	Lose 50% of your stake
Score 8-9	No gain or loss
Score 10-11	Get back stake plus 50%
Score 12	Get back stake plus 100%

After one wager, turn to **203**.

135

Becoming an initiate of Tyrnai gives you the benefit of paying less for blessings and other services the temple can offer. To qualify as an initiate you must have a COMBAT score of at least 6. Unlike other temples, there is no entry fee. You cannot become an initiate of Tyrnai if you are already an initiate of another deity.

If you choose to become an initiate (and meet the qualification) write *Tyrnai* in the God box on your Adventure Sheet. Once you have finished here, turn to **43**.

136

"Unclean!" warns the man, his voice just a ragged croak issuing from a mouth ravaged by sores. You are horrified by the realization that you have strayed into a village of lepers! Roll a die:

Score 1-3	You contract the disease; lose 1 point from each of your abilities (CHARISMA, etc.) down to a minimum score of 1
Score 4-6	You are not affected

Remember that if you have a blessing of the goddess Maka, you can use it to negate the effect of the disease.

Stay in the hamlet overnight	turn to **182**
Hurry on your way	turn to **159**

137

A flare of green light emanates from the gem. Icy cold pain stabs through your bones. Lose 1–6 points (the roll of one die) from your MAGIC score, down to a minimum score of 1.

Reeling from the psychic shock, you stumble off in blind panic until you reach the edge of the woods. Turn to **23**.

138

You can unlock the door of the black tower using a **key of stars** if you have it, or by making a THIEVERY roll at a Difficulty of 13.

Open the door	turn to **69**
Fail THIEVERY roll	turn to **92**
Go back the way you came	turn to **22**

139

You stagger on, dashing the branches aside in your desperate search for a way out of this accursed wood. Roll two dice:

Score 2-5	Ensnared in a web	turn to **208**
Score 6-7	Ominous silence	turn to **93**
Score 8-9	Elfin japes	turn to **231**
Score 10-12	A jeweled serpent	turn to **254**

140

You are on the coastal road that snakes along the windswept clifftops between Ringhorn port and the market town of Metriciens. Roll two dice:

Score 2-5	Attacked by highwaymen	turn to **702**
Score 6	An uneventful journey	turn to **353**
Score 7-12	You meet a militia patrol	turn to **409**

141

The crew welcomes you aboard your vessel with a rousing cheer. "All's shipshape, Cap'n!" declares the first mate.

Go ashore	turn to **2**
Set sail	turn to **187**

142

From Wishport, you have the option to put to sea, take the road to Haggart's Corner, or travel cross-country. In order to go by sea, you must either possess a ship which is docked in the harbor (check the Ship's Manifest) or find a captain who is willing to take you as a passenger.

Go to the harbor	turn to **325**
Take the road north	turn to **263**
Go west toward Metriciens	turn to **101**
Go east into the Magwort Fens	turn to **219**

143

If you have the codeword *Bounty*, delete it and turn to **601**. If not, turn to **625**.

144

You sail downriver until you reach Delpton. You can disembark here or remain on board as the boat heads further south.

Get out at Delpton	turn to **6**
Continue downriver	turn to **121**

THE SHOPS of CONFLASS

145

Conflass market consists of tiers of shops, linked by walkways, surrounding a pleasant green park in the middle of the town.

Armor	To buy	To sell
Leather (Defense +1)	50 Shards	45 Shards
Ring mail (Defense +2)	100 Shards	90 Shards
Chain mail (Defense +3)	—	180 Shards
Splint armor (Defense +4)	—	360 Shards
Plate armor (Defense +5)	—	720 Shards
Heavy plate (Defense +6)	—	1440 Shards

Weapons (sword, axe, etc)	To buy	To sell
Without COMBAT bonus	50 Shards	40 Shards
COMBAT bonus +1	—	200 Shards
COMBAT bonus +2	—	400 Shards
COMBAT bonus +3	—	800 Shards

Magical equipment	To buy	To sell
Amber wand (MAGIC +1)	—	400 Shards
Ebony wand (MAGIC +2)	—	800 Shards
Cobalt wand (MAGIC +3)	—	1600 Shards

Other items	To buy	To sell
Lockpicks (THIEVERY +1)	300 Shards	270 Shards
Holy symbol (SANCTITY +1)	200 Shards	100 Shards
Compass (SCOUTING +1)	—	450 Shards
Rope	50 Shards	45 Shards
Lantern	100 Shards	90 Shards

Items with no purchase price listed are not available locally. When you've finished your business here, turn to **191**.

146

You arrive at the warehouses in Ringhorn. The trick is to buy goods in an area where they are plentiful (and therefore cheap) and transport them to an area where they are in demand.

Prices are quoted here for entire Cargo Units. You cannot carry this large a quantity in person; you will need a ship to transport it.

Cargo	To buy	To sell
Furs	150 Shards	135 Shards
Grain	100 Shards	90 Shards
Metals	750 Shards	675 Shards
Minerals	625 Shards	562 Shards
Spices	900 Shards	810 Shards
Textiles	180 Shards	162 Shards
Timber	250 Shards	225 Shards

When you have completed your business here, turn to **255**.

147

The road to the coast carries a constant traffic of trade goods to and from the hinterland.

Roll two dice for encounters:

Score 2-6	A merchant caravan	turn to **524**
Score 7	An uneventful journey	turn to **287**
Score 8-12	Sokaran traders	turn to **549**

148

The temple of Alvir and Valmir is a white marble building with a wide portico which gives a panoramic view of the harbor. The air in the nave is cool and fresh after the blazing sunshine outside.

Alvir and Valmir are the twin gods responsible for storms at sea. Sailors believe they take the souls of the drowned down to their halls beneath the vasty deep.

Become an initiate	turn to **132**
Renounce worship of the twin gods	turn to **155**
Seek a blessing	turn to **178**
Leave the temple	turn to **48**

149

You mention your eerie experience on the cobblestone highway near Castle Ravayne. The abbot seems sceptical. "I am not sure that the spirits of the dead can truly speak to the living. Perhaps you dreamed the entire episode."

"If so, it is a remarkable coincidence," chips in one of the monks. "A man wearing a velvet eye patch passed through here a while ago. He said that a lucky stroke of fate had saved him from the gallows."

"Where was he bound?" you ask.

"East. To Caran Baru in Sokara, I think."

Get the codeword *Barnacle* and turn to **28**.

150

The town of Haggart's Corner stands at a place where three roads meet. Here, in certain seasons of the year, the trau are said to come and trade their marvelous trinkets in exchange for human favors.

Stop at Haggart's Corner	turn to **242**
Continue on your journey	turn to **173**

151

You have a sneaking suspicion that the priests of Sig were behind the robbery, but you cannot prove it. There is no point in reporting this incident to the City Watch—they are paid well by the priests of Sig to turn a blind eye.

Remember to cross off the money (or possession) that was stolen, then turn to **2**.

152

You pound the hydra with blow after blow. It battles on ferociously, oblivious of pain.

Hydra, COMBAT 6, Defense 7, Stamina 9

If you kill it, turn to **361**.

153

You are in open country in southeastern Golnir, close to the border with Sokara that is marked out by the River Grimm.

Go north	turn to **176**
Go east to the river	turn to **260**
Go west	turn to **196**
Go south	turn to **219**

154

Lose the codeword *Eldritch* if you have it.

You can invest money in multiples of 100 Shards. The guild will buy and sell commodities on your behalf using this money until you return to collect it. "Be advised that investments can go down in value as well as up," a guild trader reminds you.

Write the sum you are investing in the box here—or withdraw a sum invested previously. Then turn to **191**.

Money invested

155

To renounce the worship of Alvir and Valmir, you must pay 30 Shards in compensation to the priesthood. A merchant standing beside you catches your arm and shakes his head. "If you want my advice, you'll stay an initiate. I left the temple, and the following week half my fleet was wrecked in a storm off Knucklebones Point!"

Do you want to reconsider? If you are determined to renounce your faith, pay the 30 Shards and delete *Alvir and Valmir* from the God box on your Adventure Sheet. When you have finished here, turn to **148**.

156

Becoming an initiate of Alvir and Valmir gives you the benefit of paying less for blessings and other services the temple can offer. It costs 40 Shards to become an initiate. You cannot do this if you are already an initiate of another temple.

If you become an initiate, write *Alvir and Valmir* in the God box on your Adventure Sheet—and remember to cross off the 40 Shards. Once you have finished here, turn to **4**.

157

The back room of the temple is shrouded in gloom. A golden wheel is set into the far wall. You may spin this wheel once at a cost of 20 Shards. Roll one die for the outcome.

1	Lose 1 point from any ability (minimum score of 1)
2	Gain 1 point on any attribute (maximum score of 12)
3	Lose 1–6 points of Stamina *permanently*
4	Gain 1 point of Stamina *permanently*
5	Displeasure of the goddess (lose *all* blessings)
6	Favor of the goddess (write the title *Beloved of the Three Fortunes* on your Adventure Sheet)

You may not take any ability (COMBAT, CHARISMA, etc.) below 1. If your Stamina drops below 1 you are killed. Once you have spun the wheel, turn to **19**.

158

To renounce the worship of Tyrnai, you must pay 50 Shards to the priest. This purchases his intercession with the god on your behalf, so that Tyrnai does not strike you down.

If you renounce your initiate status, pay the 50 Shards and delete *Tyrnai* from the God box on your Adventure Sheet. If you had arranged a resurrection here earlier, it is canceled with no refund. When you have finished, turn to **43**.

159

A small village of cottages with thatched roofs nestles under the branches of the trees. Beside the village, a path snakes off into the gloomy woods. Not far off, several bald peasants stop work and lean on their spades to watch you.

Talk to the peasants	turn to **205**
Go along the path	turn to **228**
Strike out for fresh pastures	turn to **23**

160 ❏

If the box above is empty, put a checkmark in it now and turn to **183**. If the box is marked and you have a **key of stars**, turn to **206**. If the box is marked and you are not carrying the **key of stars**, turn to **275**.

161

The wolf crouches at the foot of the stairs and watches you with luminous green eyes. If you have a **green medallion**, turn to **230**. If not turn to **207**.

162

You emerge from the woods. Not far off to your right, you see smoke rising from the chimneys of a few crude cottages. A man wrapped in sackcloth stumbles about gathering wood.

Approach the man	turn to **136**
Continue on your way	turn to **23**

163

The voyage from Metriciens to Ringhorn is uneventful. The sky is a palette of blues and grays, the sea barely ruffled by a mild landward breeze. "In truth, I wonder why you didn't go by road," says the captain. "Not that I mind taking your money, of course." After a few days you put into Ringhorn harbor. Turn to **2**.

164

The first mate peers dourly along the dock, shaking his head at the merchants checking their wares before loading. "The lubbers!" he spits. "I'll be glad to get out o' this dump."

Go ashore	turn to **48**
Set sail	turn to **210**

165

A visit to Wheatfields market is a noisy bustling affair. You force your way through crowds of farmers who have come to trade their cattle. Outside the taverns, merchants from the south lean eagerly across the tables as they discuss the year's grain prices.

Armor	To buy	To sell
Leather (Defense +1)	50 Shards	45 Shards
Ring mail (Defense +2)	100 Shards	90 Shards
Chain mail (Defense +3)	200 Shards	180 Shards
Splint armor (Defense +4)	—	360 Shards
Plate armor (Defense +5)	—	720 Shards
Heavy plate (Defense +6)	—	1440 Shards

Weapons (sword, axe, etc)	To buy	To sell
Without COMBAT bonus	50 Shards	40 Shards
COMBAT bonus +1	250 Shards	200 Shards
COMBAT bonus +2	—	400 Shards
COMBAT bonus +3	—	800 Shards

Magical equipment	To buy	To sell
Amber wand (MAGIC +1)	—	400 Shards
Ebony wand (MAGIC +2)	—	800 Shards
Cobalt wand (MAGIC +3)	—	1600 Shards

Other items	To buy	To sell
Lockpicks (THIEVERY +1)	300 Shards	270 Shards
Holy symbol (SANCTITY +1)	200 Shards	100 Shards
Fairy mead	—	80 Shards

Items which do not have a purchase price given are not available here. When you have completed your transactions, turn to **71**.

166

An old straight road, once used by the legions of Uttaku when they marched north to wreak devastation, stretches between Castle Ravayne and Wheatfields. Now the Uttakin are long gone. Grass stalks protrude through the old cobblestones and birds chirp in the trees on either side of the road.

Roll two dice for encounters:

Score 2-8	A storyteller	turn to **447**
Score 9-12	An uneventful journey	turn to **374**

167

Marmorek is a depot town where the prospectors who mine the foothills come to buy supplies. Gray stone-built dwellings huddle under roofs made of slate tiles.

Visit the market	turn to **493**
Leave Marmorek	turn to **190**

168

You come to Conflass, a thriving market town at the point where the two rivers meet.

Visit the town	turn to **191**
Take the road west	turn to **214**
Follow the River Grimm north	turn to **99**
Follow the Rainbow River north	turn to **237**
Follow the river south	turn to **260**

169

You approach the captain of a two-masted merchantman. He looks you up and down and rubs his jaw thoughtfully. "Where are you bound?" he asks. You soon discover that passage to Dweomer or Marlock City will cost you 10 Shards, while passage to either Yellowport or Aku costs 15 Shards. You can pay the fare and set sail at once, or give up and review your other options instead.

Set sail for Yellowport	turn to **307**
Set sail for Dweomer	turn to **261**
Set sail for Aku	turn to **238**
Set sail for Marlock City	turn to **215**
Don't put to sea yet	turn to **255**

170

You pass rumbling ox-drawn carts and mule trains laden with grain and cloth. Much trade passes up and down this road.

Roll two dice for encounters:

Score 2-6	A questing knight	turn to **574**
Score 7	An uneventful journey	turn to **31**
Score 8-12	A troubled farmer	turn to **598**

171

You can leave possessions and money here to prevent having to carry them around with you. Write in the box anything you're leaving here. Each time you return, roll two dice:

Score 2-8	Your possessions are safe
Score 9-10	A thief; all the money you left here is gone
Score 11-12	A gang of burglars; lose all possessions you left here

You can also rest at your town house for as long as you wish. If injured, restore your Stamina to its normal unwounded score.

Items in town house

When you've finished at your town house, turn to **48**.

172

You are probably glad to be heading out of the Haunted Hills. Many a traveler before you has left his bones moldering there.

Head west	turn to **259**
Head east	turn to **30**
Head north	turn to **372**
Head south	turn to **328**

173

The sleepy, whimsical air of Haggart's Corner is soon forgotten as you turn your face to the wind and journey onward.

Take the road to Metriciens	turn to **216**
Take the road to the Monastery of Molhern	turn to **329**
Take the road to Wishport	turn to **263**

174

Recover the money that the assassins stole. You decline to take the deviltooth knives they were using, but you can take a **scarab amulet** and a **leather jerkin (Defense +1)**. Then turn to **2**.

175

Seeing the fearful looks of the crew, you ask the first mate what the matter is. "These are haunted waters, Cap'n!" is all he will tell you. Roll two dice:

Score 2-4	Storm	turn to **583**
Score 5-6	Pirates	turn to **587**
Score 7-10	Uneventful journey	turn to **198**
Score 11-12	The Ship of Souls	turn to **785**

176

You reach a road running from east to west. A passing peddler tells you that it is the road to Conflass.

Follow the road	turn to **214**
Go north	turn to **123**
Go south	turn to **306**

177

To find out how your investments have done, roll two dice. Add 1 to the dice roll if you are an initiate of the Three Fortunes. Also add 1 if you have the codeword *Eldritch*.

Score 2-4	Loss of 40%
Score 5-6	Loss of 20%
Score 7	No change in investment
Score 8-9	Profit of 10%
Score 10-11	Profit of 25%
Score 12-13	Profit of 50%
Score 14	Profit of 75%

Now turn to **154**, where you can withdraw the sum written in the box there after adjusting it according to the result rolled.

178

If you are an initiate it costs only 5 Shards to appease the twin gods of the sea. A non-initiate must pay 30 Shards.

Cross off the money and mark *Safety from Storms* in the Blessings box on your Adventure Sheet. The blessing works by allowing you to ignore any *one* storm at sea. When you use the blessing, cross it off your Adventure Sheet.

You can have only one Safety from Storms blessing at any time. Once it is used up, you can return to any branch of the temple of Alvir and Valmir to buy a new one.

When you are finished here, turn to **148**.

179

To renounce the worship of Alvir and Valmir, you must pay 30 Shards in compensation to the priesthood. The priests advise you not to put to sea for a while after renouncing your initiate's vows—in case the twin gods are angered by your faithlessness.

Do you want to reconsider? If you are determined to renounce your faith, pay the 30 Shards and delete *Alvir and Valmir* from the God box on your Adventure Sheet. When you have finished here, turn to **4**.

180

"Surround yourself with the symbols of luck," you overhear a priestess saying to a supplicant. "Then the threefold goddess shall smile on you."

If you have a **rabbit's foot charm**, turn to **226**. If not, turn to **203**.

181

If you are an initiate it costs only 10 Shards to purchase Tyrnai's blessing. A non-initiate must pay 25 Shards.

Cross off the money and mark *COMBAT* in the Blessings box on your Adventure Sheet. The blessing works by allowing you to try again when you make a failed COMBAT roll. It is only good for *one* re-roll. When you use the blessing, cross it off your Adventure Sheet.

You can only have one COMBAT blessing at any one time. Once it is used up, you can return to any branch of the temple of Tyrnai to buy a new one.

When you are finished here, turn to **43**.

182

You show the lepers you are not afraid to stay among them. They are grateful for your help with various chores that they find difficult. Gain 1 point of SANCTITY.

The next day you set out on your way once more. As you go, one of the lepers warns you: "In that direction lies the village of the Bald Ones. Don't trust them—they'd as soon slit your throat as look at you. The path by their village leads to the heart of the woods."

Turn to **159**.

183

The interior of the tomb is lighted by a grayish glow. A corpse in ancient knightly regalia lies on a stone slab. Awakened by your approach, it sits up. Cobwebs veil its eye sockets and its skin looks like the bark of a dead tree. It extends an accusing finger.

"For disturbing my slumber I should strike you dead where you stand," it intones in a grave voice. "But there is a way for you to earn a reprieve."

Turn and run	turn to **298**
Wait to hear what it suggests	turn to **46**

184

It was no ordinary wolf, but some sort of enchanted beast with the power of regeneration. Under your very eyes the splintered bones are knitting together, the blood pouring back through its wounds, the torn pelt becoming whole again. If you tarry here too long you will have to fight it all over again.

Climb the stairs	turn to **253**
Leave the tower	turn to **22**

185

A sprawling single-story cottage squats incongrously amid the thick black tree trunks. In front is a well from which a man in a homespun tunic is raising water. Hearing you approach, he turns and greets you cautiously.

"I am Knocklar the hermit," he says. "I don't get all that many visitors here in the Forest of the Forsaken. Are you lost?"

If you have a **severed head**, turn to **369**. If not, turn to **381**.

186

He tells a story of a woodcutter who fell asleep one afternoon and awoke to find it was dark. Having lost his way he was very frightened, but then he saw smoke over the treetops. Going on, he reached a camp where slim young gypsy maidens were dancing around a fire. With smiles and merry laughs, they invited the woodcutter to join them. Now it so happened that the woodcutter's grandmother had been a gypsy, and she'd taught him the traditional greeting which he now called out: "Dza devlesa!" which is to say, "May the gods be with you!" No sooner had the maidens heard this than they all collapsed like matchwood and, creeping closer, the woodcutter saw that there were just piles of moldering bones in the clearing, and not living people at all.

"So you know what he did?" concludes the storyteller. "He climbed an oak tree and stayed there shivering until dawn, because he knew that no ghost can follow you up an oak tree."

The day is wearing on, and it is time you were on your way. Get the codeword *Bones* and turn to **374**.

187

Sailing in coastal waters is safer but slower than out on the open ocean. Roll two dice:

Score 2-4	Storm	turn to **434**
Score 5-6	Pirates	turn to **410**
Score 7	An uneventful voyage	turn to **335**
Score 8-9	A ship of wizards	turn to **707**
Score 10-12	Mermaids	turn to **612**

188

The guild here in Wheatfields does not only organize banking facilities for its members. It also stimulates trade by putting buyers and sellers in contact with each other. You soon learn that the best buys locally are grain and furs. Acquire the codeword *Brush*.

Make an investment	turn to **49**
Check on investments	turn to **107**
Deposit or withdraw money	turn to **36**
Return to the town center	turn to **71**

189

You soon leave Chard's inn behind in your haste to seek fresh adventures.

Take the road north to Wheatfields	turn to **166**
Take the road south to Castle Ravayne	turn to **304**
Head west cross-country	turn to **75**
Head east cross-country	turn to **98**

190

The cost of passage on a boat heading downriver is 5 Shards. A barge here conveys passengers over to the west bank of the Rese at a cost of 1 Shard. Alternatively you can swim across by making a SCOUTING roll at a Difficulty of 12. (The current is strong, and the water icy cold.)

Your other option is to set out across the open countryside —there are no roads to speak of in this wild, unforgiving landscape.

Sail downriver	turn to **144**
Swim or pay to cross the river	*The Court of Hidden Faces* **333**
Failed attempt to swim	turn to **213**
Travel north overland	turn to **236**
Travel south overland	turn to **52**
Travel east overland	turn to **259**

191

Conflass is a delightful town of white-fronted houses with brightly painted timber frames. The citizens of the town are open and friendly. As one explains to you: "We tell the baronies that we pay tax to the Sokarans, and the Sokarans that we pay tax to Castle Ravayne. So they both leave us alone. That's why you'll never find a long face in Conflass."

Visit the market	turn to **145**
Find an inn	turn to **713**
Visit the merchants' guild	turn to **131**
Leave Conflass	turn to **283**

192

Owning a ship has two advantages. First, it makes it much easier to travel around. Second, it allows you to get rich by trading goods in bulk.

Goods are transported in Cargo Units. (A Cargo Unit weighs several tons—much more than one person could carry!) The more expensive your ship, the greater its carrying capacity. More expensive ships are also more seaworthy.

Choose a ship from the types listed here.

Type	Cost	Capacity
Barque	250 Shards	1 Cargo Unit
Brigantine	450 Shards	2 Cargo Units
Galleon	900 Shards	3 Cargo Units

Record your ship in the box provided on the Ship's Manifest. You get to choose the ship's name. The crew quality is average unless you hire on better sailors. Each time you arrive at a new destination, change the entry in the Docked column to the ship's current location. (So, if you aren't going to set sail immediately, note that the ship is docked at Ringhorn.)

Hire a better crew	turn to **330**
Leave the city	turn to **370**
Visit the warehouses	turn to **146**
Return to the city center	turn to **2**

193

An inn with low overhanging eaves nestles in the side of a hill beside the bleak Whistling Heath.

Stop at the inn	turn to **218**
Take the road north	turn to **170**
Take the road south	turn to **147**
Head west cross-country	turn to **98**
Head east over the Heath	turn to **124**

194

Metriciens market is one of the largest you have ever seen. It stretches for hundreds of yards, through piazzas covered with silk awnings, along the great esplanade overlooking the bay, and through shadowy colonnades where fortunes are made and lost in the course of a single conversation.

Armor	To buy	To sell
Leather (Defense +1)	50 Shards	45 Shards
Ring mail (Defense +2)	100 Shards	90 Shards
Chain mail (Defense +3)	200 Shards	180 Shards
Splint armor (Defense +4)	400 Shards	360 Shards
Plate armor (Defense +5)	—	720 Shards
Heavy plate (Defense +6)	—	1440 Shards

Weapons (sword, axe, etc)	To buy	To sell
Without COMBAT bonus	50 Shards	40 Shards
COMBAT bonus +1	250 Shards	200 Shards
COMBAT bonus +2	—	400 Shards
COMBAT bonus +3	—	800 Shards

Magical equipment	To buy	To sell
Amber wand (MAGIC +1)	500 Shards	400 Shards
Ebony wand (MAGIC +2)	1000 Shards	800 Shards
Cobalt wand (MAGIC +3)	—	1600 Shards

Other items	To buy	To sell
Holy symbol (SANCTITY +1)	—	30 Shards
Compass (SCOUTING +1)	500 Shards	450 Shards
Rope	50 Shards	45 Shards
Lantern	100 Shards	90 Shards
Pirate captain's head	—	150 Shards
Parchment	2 Shards	1 Shard
Fairy mead	—	250 Shards
Silver horseshoe	—	100 Shards
Rabbit's foot charm	—	100 Shards
Scarab amulet	—	100 Shards
Key of stars	—	200 Shards

Items with no purchase price listed are not available locally. When you have finished at the market, turn to **48**.

195

North of the Whistling Heath lie fertile lands that provide rich pickings for the yeomen of central Golnir. Roll two dice:

Score 2-7	Uneventful journey	turn to **200**
Score 8-12	A damsel in distress	turn to **599**

196

A dismal tract of chalk-hued moorland dotted with dusk-colored heather lies north of the fell Magwort Fens. Roll two dice:

Score 2-6	A vagabond with a tale	turn to **743**
Score 7-8	Uneventful journey	turn to **246**
Score 9-12	A troll with three heads	turn to **767**

197

Becoming an initiate of Alvir and Valmir gives you the benefit of paying less for blessings and other services the temple can offer. It costs 40 Shards to become an initiate. You cannot do this if you are already an initiate of another temple.

If you choose to become an initiate, write *Alvir and Valmir* in the God box on your Adventure Sheet—and remember to cross off the 40 Shards. Once you have finished here, turn to **301**.

198

You are at sea off Knucklebones Point.

Go west	turn to **210**
Go east	turn to **119**
Go south	*Over the Blood-Dark Sea* **402**

199

You are traveling cross-country in eastern Golnir, in the rolling hills that sweep down toward the broad river valley of the Grimm. A horse trader tells you that the town of Goldfall is close at hand. "See this scar on my forehead?" he says, pulling off his straw hat. "A nugget fell from the sky and hit me, so it did! But a villain made off with my nugget while I lay stretched out senseless on the grass."

Travel to Goldfall	turn to **81**
Travel to Wheatfields	turn to **71**
Go south	turn to **333**
Make for the River Grimm	turn to **176**

200

You are traveling through a region of fields and pastures in central Golnir.

Go east	turn to **333**
Go south to the Whistling Heath	turn to **124**
Go west	turn to **280**
Go north to Wheatfields	turn to **71**

201

Becoming an initiate of the Three Fortunes gives you the benefit of paying less for blessings and other services the temple can offer. It costs 75 Shards to become an initiate. You cannot do this if you are already an initiate of another temple.

If you choose to become an initiate, write *The Three Fortunes* in the God box on your Adventure Sheet—and remember to cross off the 75 Shards. Once you have finished here, turn to **102**.

202

If you are an initiate it costs only 5 Shards to propitiate the twin gods of the sea. A non-initiate must pay 20 Shards.

Cross off the money and mark *Safety from Storms* in the Blessings box on your Adventure Sheet. The blessing works by allowing you to ignore any *one* storm at sea. When you use the blessing, cross it off your Adventure Sheet.

You can have only one Safety from Storms blessing at a time. Once it is used up, you can return to any branch of the temple of Alvir and Valmir to buy a new one.

When you are finished here, turn to **4**.

203

The priestesses come forward to ask your business. From the back of the temple you can hear the sound of dice rattling on a wooden table.

Become an initiate of the Fortunes	turn to **42**
Renounce their worship	turn to **65**
Seek a blessing	turn to **88**
Gamble	turn to **111**
Leave the temple	turn to **81**

204

Resurrection costs 200 Shards if you are an initiate, and 800 Shards if not. It is the last word in insurance. Once you have arranged for resurrection you need not fear death, as you will be magically restored to life here at the temple.

To arrange resurrection, pay the fee and write *Shrine of Tyrnai* (*Cities of Gold and Glory* 227) in the Resurrection box on your Adventure Sheet. If you are killed, turn to **227** in this book. You can have only one resurrection arranged at a time.

When you are finished here, turn to **43**.

205

The evil bald villagers pelt you with rocks, hoping to rob you. Roll two dice and subtract your armor's Defense bonus, if any. The result is how many Stamina points you lose for the stoning. If you survive, you hurry away.

Take the path into the wood	turn to **228**
Leave this region	turn to **23**

206

Suppressing a shudder, you put the glittering **key of stars** into the undead creature's hands. It gives a dry hiss of pleasure.

"Now I know my treasure is safe, I shall sleep soundly," it says.

Closing its dead gray fingers tight around the precious key, it lies back on its slab and becomes inert once more.

Attack it	turn to **275**
Quietly search the crypt	turn to **344**
Leave at once	turn to **22**

207

With a growl it leaps forward, fangs bared hungrily. You must fight.

Fairy Wolf, COMBAT 5, Defense 7, Stamina 10

Because the fairy wolf is chained to the wall, you can flee from combat at any time, but you will take a final wound of 1–6 Stamina points (roll one die for how many) as you run away from the creature.

Fight and kill the wolf	turn to **184**
Flee from the tower	turn to **22**

208

You are caught in a web whose strands are as thick as a trawler's net.

Feeling the warning of your sixth sense, you look up into the branches in time to see a globular shape with many long hairy legs dropping silently out of the darkness.

Giant Spider, COMBAT 4, Defense 7, Stamina 5

Because you are tangled in the web, you cannot run away from this fight.

If you defeat the spider, turn to **277**.

209

You remember the old storyteller's cautionary tale. Your cheery wave attracts luring smiles from the dancers, but their smiles turn to glares of shock and rage when you greet them in the name of the gods. Flickering like candles in a breeze, they vanish from sight. Turn to **244**.

210

Your ship is hugging Golnir's southern coast. Roll two dice:

Score 2-4	Storm	turn to **484**
Score 5-6	Pirates	turn to **608**
Score 7-8	An uneventful voyage	turn to **358**
Score 9-12	A shipwrecked mariner	turn to **687**

211

You can leave possessions and money here to prevent having to carry them around with you. Write in the box anything you are leaving here. Each time you return, roll two dice:

Score 2-9	Your possessions are safe
Score 10	A thief; all the money you left here is gone
Score 11-12	A fire; your town house and all its contents have been destroyed

You can also rest at your town house for as long as you wish. If injured, restore your Stamina to its normal unwounded score. When you've finished at your town house, turn to **71** (and remember to erase the checkmark in the town house box there if it was destroyed by fire).

Items at townhouse

212

You are in the Rese Valley. Off to the east stretch the corn-rich lands of the Endless Plains. Northward, the countryside gives way to rugged foothills where human settlement is sparse.

Go north toward Marmorek	turn to **167**
Go east across the Endless Plains	turn to **328**
Go south to Delpton	turn to **6**

213

The current drags you down and your lungs fill with water. Buffeted by the torrent, you are swept downstream and flung on to a stretch of gravel. Lose 3–18 Stamina (the score of three dice). If alive, you can slog back to town. Turn to **190**.

214

You follow the twisting dirt road that lies between the River of Souls and the Monastery of Molhern, God of Artisans and Scholars. Miraculously you see no living soul on your journey —even though many pilgrims must use this route. Perhaps the legend is true: "Each must find his own path to the light of Molhern." Turn to **240**.

215

You sail out of Ringhorn toward Marlock City. Roll two dice:

Score 2-5	Storm at sea	turn to **781**
Score 6-12	Nothing troublesome	*The War-Torn Kingdom* **240**

216

You are on a road that stretches across the downs between Haggart's Corner and the coast.

Roll two dice for encounters:

Score 2-6	Wandering priests	turn to **622**
Score 7-8	Uneventful journey	turn to **127**
Score 9-12	Knights of Nagil	turn to **646**

217

Wishport is a picturesque town set at the back of a bay rimmed by white cliffs. Fish, oil, dyes, and other commodities are packed here for transport inland. You can buy a town house here for 100 Shards. If you decide to, cross off the money and put a checkmark in the box by the town house option.

Visit the market	turn to **302**
Visit the harbor	turn to **325**
Lodge at an inn	turn to **737**
Visit the merchants' guild	turn to **3**
Visit your town house ❑ (if box marked)	turn to **348**
Visit the temple of Alvir and Valmir	turn to **4**
Visit the temple of the Three Fortunes	turn to **27**
Leave Wishport	turn to **142**

218

A sign hanging outside the inn proclaims: *Civilization stops here!* "Surely you risk offending travelers coming from the other direction," you say to the innkeeper, a friendly man named Troilus.

With a beaming smile, he leads you to the other side of the sign. The same words are written there. "I flatter everyone, offend no one. It is a good philosophy of life."

Troilus charges 1 Shard a day for board and lodging. Each day you spend here, you can recover 1 Stamina point if injured, up to the limit of your normal unwounded Stamina score. When you are ready to leave, turn to **241**.

219

Flat, waterlogged ground surrounds you in all directions. A few trees stretch forlornly into the sky above banks of reeds. These are the Magwort Fens.

Make a SCOUTING roll at a Difficulty of 13.

Successful SCOUTING roll	turn to **465**
Failed SCOUTING roll	turn to **464**

220

To renounce the worship of Alvir and Valmir, you must pay 30 Shards in compensation to the priesthood. The high priest shakes his head sadly. "I beg you to reconsider," he urges. "All too often I have seen initiates renounce the twin gods, only to suffer calamity at sea within days or weeks."

Do you want to change your mind? If you are determined to renounce your faith, pay the 30 Shards and delete *Alvir and Valmir* from the God box on your Adventure Sheet. When you have finished here, turn to **301**.

221

"It's slow going so close to land," mutters the helmsman. "Are you sure you don't want me to steer out to sea, skipper?"

Head west	turn to **187**
Head east	turn to **210**
Steer south	*Over the Blood-Dark Sea* **301**

222

You are traveling in southwest Golnir, somewhere between Metriciens and Castle Ravayne.

Head south to the coastal road	turn to **373**
Go north	turn to **98**
Travel to Castle Ravayne	turn to **25**
Head toward the Whistling Heath	turn to **124**
Go due east from here	turn to **245**

223

You are in open country southeast of the Whistling Heath. There ought to be some roads around here somewhere.

Head east	turn to **150**
Head south to the coast	turn to **48**
Head up on to the heath	turn to **124**

224

To renounce the worship of the Three Fortunes, you must pay 25 Shards to the priesthood by way of compensation. The priestess listens placidly while you explain that you no longer want to be an initiate.

"So you wish to abandon luck, fortune, and destiny," she says. Is she smiling? You cannot tell because of the gold-threaded veil the Fortunes' priestesses all wear.

Do you want to reconsider? If you are determined to renounce your faith, pay the 25 Shards and delete *The Three Fortunes* from the God box on your Adventure Sheet. When you have finished here, turn to **102**.

225

Becoming an initiate of the Three Fortunes gives you the benefit of paying less for blessings and other services the temple can offer. It costs 75 Shards to become an initiate. You cannot do this if you are already an initiate of another temple.

If you choose to become an initiate, write *The Three Fortunes* in the God box on your Adventure Sheet—and remember to cross off the 75 Shards.

Once you have finished here, turn to **27**.

226

The high priestess sees the charm around your neck and smiles. "The goddesses will surely favor you," she says.

If you have a **silver horseshoe**, turn to **249**. If not, turn to **203**.

227

You are restored to life at the war god's shrine in Castle Ravayne. Your Stamina is back to its normal score. The possessions and cash you were carrying at the time of your death are lost. Cross them off your Adventure Sheet. Also remember to delete the entry in the Resurrection box now that it has been used.

Tyrnai's priest clasps your arm. "Welcome back to the land of the living," he says. "Tyrnai has seen fit to restore you so that you may send more souls to him in battle."

Turn to **43**.

228

The path leads to a grassy glade beside a brook. If you have the codeword *Baluster*, turn to **343**. If not, turn to **68**.

229

Your captors take you to Metriciens, where the payment of the ransom is arranged through the auspices of the merchants' guild. Turn to **36** and deduct the ransom demand from your account at the guild.

Not enough banked to cover the ransom	turn to **252**
Ransom paid in full	turn to **48**

230

Apparently recognizing the medallion, the wolf slinks aside and lets you climb the stairs.

Ascend to the top of the tower	turn to **253**
Leave now	turn to **22**

231

The elves are watching you, as invisible as ghosts in the foliage. They amuse themselves by cruelly rearranging your nose so that it looks like a carrot pointing straight up into the air. You can only undo this spell by making a MAGIC roll now at a Difficulty of 13. If you fail the roll, you will be the butt of ridicule for everyone you meet and you must therefore lose 1 point from your CHARISMA score.

Now turn to **93**.

232

Ringhorn market consists of hundreds of stalls crowded into a cobbled square under the walls of the Sheriff's citadel. This is where you can buy and sell personal items. Items with no purchase price listed are not available locally.

Armor	To buy	To sell
Leather (Defense +1)	50 Shards	45 Shards
Ring mail (Defense +2)	100 Shards	90 Shards
Chain mail (Defense +3)	—	180 Shards
Splint armor (Defense +4)	—	360 Shards
Plate armor (Defense +5)	—	720 Shards
Heavy plate (Defense +6)	—	1440 Shards

Weapons (sword, axe, etc)	To buy	To sell
Without COMBAT bonus	50 Shards	40 Shards
COMBAT bonus +1	—	200 Shards
COMBAT bonus +2	—	400 Shards
COMBAT bonus +3	—	800 Shards

Magical equipment	To buy	To sell
Amber wand (MAGIC +1)	—	400 Shards
Ebony wand (MAGIC +2)	—	800 Shards
Cobalt wand (MAGIC +3)	—	1600 Shards

Other items	To buy	To sell
Lockpicks (THIEVERY +1)	300 Shards	270 Shards
Holy symbol (SANCTITY +1)	200 Shards	100 Shards
Compass (SCOUTING +1)	500 Shards	450 Shards
Rope	50 Shards	45 Shards
Parchment	2 Shards	1 Shard
Lantern	100 Shards	90 Shards

For bulk trade goods you need to visit the warehouses at the waterfront. When you're through here, turn to **2**.

233

There are two advantages to owning a ship. First, it makes it much easier to travel around. Second, it allows you to get rich by trading goods in bulk. Goods are transported in Cargo Units. (A Cargo Unit weighs several tons—much more than one person could carry!) The more expensive your ship, the greater its carrying capacity. More expensive ships are also more seaworthy.

Choose a ship from the types listed here.

Type	Cost	Capacity
Barque	250 Shards	1 Cargo Unit
Brigantine	450 Shards	2 Cargo Units
Galleon	900 Shards	3 Cargo Units

Record your ship in the box provided on the Ship's Manifest. You get to choose the ship's name. The crew quality is average unless you hire on better sailors. Each time you arrive at a new destination, change the entry in the Docked column to the ship's current location. (So if you aren't going to sail right away, note that the ship is docked at Wishport.)

Hire a better crew	turn to **50**
Leave the city	turn to **142**
Visit the warehouses	turn to **96**
Return to the city center	turn to **217**

234

Maka is the dread goddess of disease and famine, who must be appeased to ensure good harvests. When Maka is angry, the crops are struck with pestilence and people go hungry. Her temple is a high-gabled building of dark wood with narrow leaded lights that admit only a dismal gloom to the interior of the nave.

Become an initiate of Maka	turn to **87**
Renounce her worship	turn to **110**
Seek a blessing	turn to **133**
Leave	turn to **71**

235

You are wandering through the pleasant countryside of southwest Golnir.

Head west toward the Rese River	turn to **120**
Head due east	turn to **280**
Head toward the Whistling Heath	turn to **193**
Head south toward the coast	turn to **78**

236

This is bleak country in the shadow of the northern foothills. Beyond rise the jagged snow-peaked mountains known as the Spine of Harkun.

Head north toward the mountains	turn to **282**
Go east	turn to **259**
Go south	turn to **52**
Head for the town of Marmorek	turn to **167**

237

You follow the course of the frothing Rainbow River as it tumbles across flat glistening stones and boulder-strewn rapids.
Roll two dice:

Score 2-6	Gypsy camp	turn to **498**
Score 7-8	An uneventful journey	turn to **371**
Score 9-12	Fishermen in a canoe	turn to **523**

238

The ship sets sail out of Ringhorn, bound for the strange nation of the Uttakin. "There's trouble on the wind, skipper," reckons the first mate. The captain's only reply is a sour grunt.
Roll two dice:

Score 2-7	Uttakin slavers	turn to **399**
Score 8-12	A trouble-free voyage	*The Court of Hidden Faces* **444**

239

The ship sails out of Metriciens harbor. On only the first day out, the quartermaster says something ominous: "I didn't like the look of those fellows watching us load the cargo. Foreign-looking types, they were."
Roll two dice:

Score 2-6	Attacked by pirates	turn to **670**
Score 7-12	Your fears are unfounded	*The War-Torn Kingdom* **140**

240

You are traveling on the stretch of road between Conflass and the remote Monastery of Molhern.

Go west to the monastery	turn to **94**
Go east to Conflass	turn to **168**
Leave the road and travel north	turn to **123**
Strike off to the south	turn to **306**

241

You travel on, leaving behind the inn and the desolate windswept expanse of the heaths.

Take the road north to Wheatfields	turn to **170**
Take the road south to Metriciens	turn to **147**

242

Haggart's Corner is a pretty, pastel-hued town. Houses with high gables and bay windows are set around a series of courts where fountains splash dreamily in the sunlight.

Ask about trade with the Trau	turn to **782**
Go to the market	turn to **779**
Visit the temple of Lacuna	turn to **294**
Lodge at an inn	turn to **761**
Leave Haggart's Corner	turn to **173**

243

If you are an initiate it costs only 5 Shards to gain the blessing of the twin gods of the sea. A non-initiate must pay 20 Shards. Cross off the money and mark *Safety from Storms* in the Blessings box on your Adventure Sheet. The blessing works by allowing you to ignore any *one* storm at sea. When you use the blessing, cross it off your Adventure Sheet.

You can only have one Safety from Storms blessing at any one time. Once it is used up, you can return to any branch of the temple of Alvir and Valmir to buy a new one.

When you are finished here, turn to **2**.

244

Under the carpet of dead leaves you find some shallow graves filled with yellow skeletons. Each has dried blood on its jaws. You break branches off an oak tree, sharpen them into stakes, and drive one through the rib cage of each skeleton. Only then do you feel safe enough to search the graves thoroughly, discovering 200 Shards in old coins. Add this to your money and then turn to **349**.

245

You come to a road running north-south. A wandering entertainer stands nearby changing the wheel of his cart. He tells you that the road runs between Wheatfields and Metriciens. "Both cities are dens of traducers, venifers, and sundry other callid rascals," he says resentfully. "I advise you to shun them, those edacious fustilugs in their gaudy baudekins!"

Go east	turn to **54**
Go west	turn to **78**
Take the road north toward Wheatfields	turn to **193**
Go south to Metriciens	turn to **48**

246

You are wandering across a patch of moorland east of Haggart's Corner.

Go south into the fens	turn to **219**
Go west to Haggart's Corner	turn to **150**
Strike out east toward the river	turn to **306**

247

If you are an initiate it costs only 20 Shards to purchase The Three Fortunes' blessing. A non-initiate must pay 80 Shards.

Cross off the money and mark *Luck* in the Blessings box on your Adventure Sheet. The blessing works by allowing you to re-roll any dice result *once*. (This does not have to be an ability roll. You could also use it to re-roll an encounter result that you didn't want.) When you use the blessing, cross it off your Adventure Sheet.

You can only have one Luck blessing at any one time.

Once it is used up, you can return to any branch of the temple of The Three Fortunes to buy a new one.

When you are finished here, turn to **102**.

248

Mischievous elfin fingers delve into your haversack when you aren't looking. You must lose 1–6 possessions (roll a die to see how many). The items stolen are the ones listed first on your Adventure Sheet. If you have the codeword *Bosky*, turn to **300**. If not, turn to **93**.

249

The worshippers of the Three Fortunes admire you as a paragon of the faith. "You are an example to us all," says a bent-backed old prospector with a gold tooth. If you have a **four-leaf clover**, turn to **272**. If not, turn to **203**.

250

The guards recognize you as a champion of the noble house of Ravayne. They salute as you go into the keep. Turn to **342**.

251

You lash out, knocking the dwarf to the ground. As he sits cradling his head, you hurry over to the figure on horseback. As you lift the visor, a wisp of green smoke curls out and you hear a voice say: "I thank you, mortal, for my freedom."

The smoke disperses on the breeze: the armor is empty.

Get the codewords *Bosky* and *Baluster*. You can also take **plate armor (Defense +5)** and a **curved sword (COMBAT +1)**, since the dwarf is in no state to stop you.

Continue along the path	turn to **343**
Turn back	turn to **23**

252

Your body is found floating face down under the boardwalk leading to the shipyards. If you have resurrection arranged, turn to the section noted on your Adventure Sheet. Otherwise your great adventuring career has come to a rather ignoble end.

253 ❑

At the top of the staircase you come to a belfry filled with roosting vampire bats that hang like sacks of dun-colored leather around a vast iron bell. A loathsome trickle of fleas and lice falls constantly from the bats' fur.

If the box above is not marked, mark it now and turn to **276**. If the box is already marked, turn to **299**.

254 ❑

If the box above is not marked, mark it now and turn to **580**. If the box is already marked, turn to **604**.

255

At the harbor of Ringhorn you can buy a ship—or put one to sea, if you already have a ship docked at this location.

While you are here it is also possible to visit the warehouses lining the waterfront, where goods from afar are bought and sold in quantity.

Buy a ship	turn to **192**
Sell a ship	turn to **284**
Go aboard your ship	turn to **141**
Hire crew for your ship	turn to **330**
Pay for passage on a ship	turn to **169**
Visit the warehouses	turn to **146**
Return to the city center	turn to **2**

RINGHORN HARBOUR

256

You can get the following price for a secondhand ship:

Type	Sale price
Barque	210 Shards
Brigantine	400 Shards
Galleon	800 Shards

Remember to cross the ship off the Ship's Manifest if you go ahead with the sale. When you have finished your business here, turn to **325**.

257

The temple of Nagil here in Wheatfields is decorated with wall carvings showing sheafs of fresh corn. "Most think of Nagil as the death god," explains a priest, "but of course he is more than that. For in nature, how can there be rebirth and growth without death?"

Become an initiate of Nagil	turn to **362**
Renounce his worship	turn to **18**
Make resurrection arrangements	turn to **41**
Leave the temple	turn to **71**

258

You can head south to Ringhorn, or north to Castle Ravayne and beyond.

Travel to Ringhorn	turn to **2**
Travel to Castle Ravayne	turn to **25**

259

Wind whistles across a wide expanse of heathland dotted with just a few scattered villages. To the north, half hidden in the murk of low clouds, looms the snow-peaked mountain range known as the Spine of Harkun.

Head east toward the Haunted Hills	turn to **305**
Head north toward the mountains	turn to **282**
Travel west	turn to **236**
Travel south	turn to **328**

260

You are walking along the bank of the River Grimm—called the River of Souls because it is said to carry ghost barges laden with the souls of the dead. Roll two dice:

Score 2-6	Travelers from Sokara	turn to **548**
Score 7-8	An uneventful journey	turn to **130**
Score 9-12	River Wraiths	turn to **573**

261

The ship maneuvers out of the harbor and on to the open sea. "We'll have no trouble on this voyage," announces the captain. "I took the precaution of buying a charm of protection from Fortuity College in Dweomer."

Whether it is the power of the charm or simple good luck, the journey is indeed without mishap and a few days later you dock at Dweomer. Turn to **100** in *Over the Blood-Dark Sea*.

262

The voyage from Metriciens to Marlock City takes only a few days. You are amazed that it passes without incident, until the captain tells you: "I pay a regular tribute to the Reavers. They don't need to intercept my ship to get money out of me."

Turn to **240** in *The War-Torn Kingdom*.

263

The road follows the ridge of low hills extending out into the headland of Knucklebones Point.

Roll two dice for encounters:

Score 2-5	Eerie things	turn to **400**
Score 6-8	Uneventful journey	turn to **288**
Score 9-12	Penniless adventurers	turn to **450**

264

The boat takes you upriver as far as Castle Ravayne, a journey of several days. You can disembark here or stay onboard and travel further upriver.

Visit Castle Ravayne	turn to **25**
Journey upriver	turn to **281**
Disembark and go west	*The Court of Hidden Faces* **222**

265

You are on the road between Haggart's Corner and the Monastery of Molhern.

Follow the road to Haggart's Corner	turn to **150**
Follow the road to the monastery	turn to **94**
Venture south off the road	turn to **196**
Strike out cross-country to the west	turn to **54**

266

You sail out of Wishport toward Marlock City. Only a few days out, the crew begins to succumb to fever. Soon the ship is drifting unmanned while most of the sailors lie groaning below deck. You catch the fever yourself and must *permanently* lose 1–3 Stamina points (roll one die and halve the result, rounding fractions up). If you have the blessing of Immunity to Disease and Poison you can ignore this. Remember to cross the blessing off your Adventure Sheet.

If you survive, eventually enough men recover to sail the ship on to its destination. Turn to **240** in *The War-Torn Kingdom*.

267

If you are fighting with a sword, axe, or katana, turn to **313**. Otherwise turn to **152**.

268

You are on the headland that stretches out to Knucklebones Point.

Go south to the coast	turn to **291**
Go west to Metriciens	turn to **48**
Go east to Wishport	turn to **217**
Go north to Haggart's Corner	turn to **150**

269

"Welcome, dear friend," says the high priest in greeting. "I trust your fortune grows as quickly as your fame?"

Renounce the worship of Alvir and Valmir	turn to **220**
Seek a blessing	turn to **243**
Leave the temple	turn to **2**

270

Becoming an initiate of Nagil is not possible if you are already an initiate of another temple. You are made to undergo various trials to test your worthiness. In the last test, you are sealed in a casket below the ground and made to confront your own fears. To pass the tests you must roll under your Rank on one die. If successful, write *Nagil* in the God box on your Adventure Sheet. Once you have finished here, turn to **125**.

271

If you are an initiate it costs only 20 Shards to purchase The Three Fortunes' blessing. A non-initiate must pay 80 Shards.

Cross off the money and mark *Luck* in the Blessings box on your Adventure Sheet. The blessing works by allowing you to re-roll any dice result *once*. (This does not have to be an ability roll. You could also use it to re-roll an encounter result.) When you use the blessing, cross it off your Adventure Sheet.

You can have only one Luck blessing at any one time. Once it is used up, you can return to any branch of the temple of The Three Fortunes to buy a new one.

When you are finished here, turn to **27**.

272

A gaunt woman accosts you in the nave of the temple and says: "If only I had such a collection of lucky charms as you've got there."

If you decide to give her your **four-leaf clover, silver horseshoe,** and **rabbit's foot charm**, remember to cross them off your Adventure Sheet.

Give her the three items	turn to **295**
Keep them	turn to **318**

273

The guards are not convinced you are important enough to be admitted to the keep. "Has the baroness summoned you?" they demand to know. "She is very busy."

To convince them to let you in, you need to make a CHARISMA roll at a Difficulty of 10.

Successful CHARISMA roll	turn to **296**
Failed CHARISMA roll	turn to **319**
Give up and walk off	turn to **315**

274

"I'll trounce you!" sniggers the dwarf. "I mean, my master will."

With that, he waddles off toward the pavilion. You are a little surprised that he isn't going to stay and watch, since he seems so confident of the outcome.

Prepare to joust	turn to **297**
Turn back	turn to **23**

275

The corpse reaches out its skeletal hands, clutching your throat in a grip like a noose of ice. You struggle to break free, but your limbs have lost their strength. A ghastly chuckling pounds in your ears as the corpse feasts on your soul.

Attempt a SANCTITY roll at a Difficulty of 15. If the roll is successful, your spirit is too pure for the fiend to ingest; you are hurled out of the tomb with the loss of 3–18 Stamina (roll three dice). If you survive, turn to **22**. If you fail the SANCTITY roll then even resurrection cannot save you from being utterly destroyed by the vampire knight.

276

The floor of the belfry is virtually covered with silver, gold, and precious gems—all sprinkled with bat guano. Two items draw your gaze: a **golden sword (COMBAT +2)** and a **regal helm (Defense +3)**. You can take these two items; record them as possessions on your Adventure Sheet. You can also try to gather some treasure before the vampire bats wake up.

Gather some treasure	turn to **322**
Leave without further delay	turn to **22**

277

Its bite was venomous. If you were injured during the fight, lose an additional 1–6 Stamina points now. (Remember that if you have a blessing of the goddess Maka, you can use it to negate the effect of the poison.)

Assuming you survive, you search the spider's den and find several corpses wrapped up in web silk. Among the litter of moldered bones, you find 50 Shards—treasure that the spider's previous victims have no further use for. Note it on your Adventure Sheet and then turn to **93**.

278

You can leave possessions and money here to prevent having to carry them around with you. Record in the box anything you wish to leave. Each time you return, roll two dice:

Score 2-8   Your possessions are safe
Score 9-10   A thief; all the money you left here is gone
Score 11   A gang of burglars; lose all possessions you left here
Score 12   A fire; your town house and all its contents have been destroyed

You can also rest at your town house for as long as you wish. If injured, restore your Stamina to its normal unwounded score. When you've finished at your town house, turn to **2** (and remember to erase the checkmark in the town house box if it was destroyed by fire).

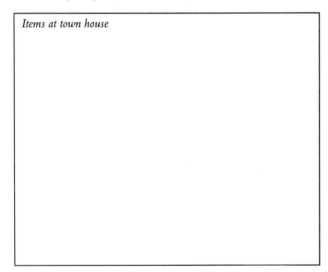

Items at town house

279

You stride up the gangplank to find the crew dancing merrily to the tune of a flute. "Ah, shkipper, jush tryin' to keep the crew trit 'n' fim," slurs the bosun as he hastily conceals a bottle of grog. You shake your head despairingly and go to your cabin. Maybe you should have hired a better crew?

Go back into town	turn to **217**
Walk along the harborfront	turn to **325**
Set sail	turn to **119**

280

You reach the road that connects Wheatfields with the port of Metriciens.

Follow the road	turn to **170**
Go east over open country	turn to **195**
Go west over open country	turn to **98**

281

The boat slowly makes its way up the Rese River. On either bank lie scattered villages. Beyond, the fertile farmlands of Golnir stretch off to the horizon. After a few days you reach the village of Delpton, where you can disembark if you wish.

Continue upriver	turn to **350**
Disembark here	turn to **6**

282

High jagged peaks tumble up to the verge of heaven. Legend has it that this mountain range is the exposed backbone of the slaughtered god Harkun. As you clamber up a steep trail, you see a waterfall gushing from high above. Something metallic glitters in the rock face where the waterfall issues out.

Climb up for a closer look	turn to **508**
Ignore it	turn to **533**

283

Your options include hiring passage on a barge going south, at a cost of 3 Shards.

Barge to Marlock City	*The War-Torn Kingdom* **240**
Follow the riverbank south	turn to **260**
Take the road west	turn to **214**
Follow the River Grimm north	turn to **99**
Follow the Rainbow River north	turn to **237**

THE SPINE of HARKUN

284

Asking around, you find the best prices that can be got for a secondhand vessel:

Type	Sale price
Barque	210 Shards
Brigantine	400 Shards
Galleon	800 Shards

If you go ahead with the sale, cross the ship off the Ship's Manifest. Turn to **255**.

285

You browse through the warehouses in Metriciens. To turn a profit you must buy goods where they are cheap and sell them where they are in demand. Prices are quoted for single Cargo Units. Such large quantities can be transported only by ship.

Cargo	To buy	To sell
Furs	210 Shards	189 Shards
Grain	90 Shards	81 Shards
Metals	850 Shards	765 Shards
Minerals	650 Shards	585 Shards
Spices	800 Shards	720 Shards
Textiles	250 Shards	225 Shards
Timber	260 Shards	234 Shards

When you have completed your business here, turn to **33**.

286

You are leaving the town of Wheatfields.

Go north to the Endless Plains	turn to **328**
Take the west road to Delpton	turn to **327**
Take the road to Castle Ravayne	turn to **166**
Take the road to Metriciens	turn to **170**
Take the east road	turn to **309**

287

You are on the road leading down to Metriciens on the coast.

Go south to Metriciens	turn to **48**
Go north toward Wheatfields	turn to **193**
Leave the road and head west	turn to **78**
Leave the road and head east	turn to **54**

288

You are on the road between Wishport and Haggart's Corner.

Follow the road to Wishport	turn to **217**
Go north to Haggart's Corner	turn to **150**
Go due south toward the coast	turn to **101**
Go east into the Magwort Fens	turn to **219**

289

The sides of the pit are funneled to prevent you from climbing out. After a while the brigands arrive, dropping a net to ensnare you. They strip you of all your possessions and cash (cross them off your Adventure Sheet). They are about to slit your throat when one of them thinks to ask if you have any money invested with the merchants' guild. "Enough to pay a ransom of 150 Shards, say?"

If you can pay a ransom of 150 Shards, turn to **229**. If not, the brigands kill you.

290

The hydra spits acid at your back. If you are wearing any armor, you have to strip it off and discard it before the acid eats through to your skin. Cross the armor off your Adventure Sheet. (If you didn't have any armor, you lose 3–18 Stamina points instead.) If you are still alive, turn to **640**.

291

Castle Orlock is a brooding fortress encased behind walls of weathered black granite. The interior is unlit, and in order to explore you must have a **lantern** or **candle**.

Enter the castle	turn to **440**
Go on your way	turn to **314**

292

"You do not have to be an initiate to worship here," intones a priest, "but it makes the temple's services that much cheaper."

Become an initiate of Alvir and Valmir	turn to **197**
Seek a blessing	turn to **243**
Leave	turn to **2**

293

You tell the high priest that you wish to renounce the worship of Nagil. He summons four acolytes bearing a pall and asks you to lie on it so that they can carry you outside. When you ask what this symbolizes, he gives a faint shrug and says, "You must draw your own conclusion."

Do you want to reconsider? If you are determined to renounce your faith, delete *Nagil* from the God box on your Adventure Sheet. You must lose any outstanding resurrection arrangements, and also the title *Chosen One of Nagil* if you have it. When you have finished here, turn to **125**.

294

Lacuna is the moon goddess and the overseer of the hunt. She is the patron deity of woodsmen, hunters, and those who walk in the wild corners of the world.

Her temple here in Haggart's Corner is a simple log-built chapel with bronze shields set along the walls. Grass carpets the floor and there is a smell of heather in the air. Pine cones smolder on the altar.

Become an initiate of Lacuna	turn to **317**
Renounce her worship	turn to **340**
Seek a blessing	turn to **363**
Leave	turn to **242**

295

You don't see what happens to the woman. She was right behind you as you approached the altar, but when you turn around she is nowhere to be seen.

Gain 1 point of SANCTITY for your generosity to the woman, then turn to **203**.

296

The guards are convinced by your persuasive tongue. One of them gestures with his thumb, saying, "Go on in, then, before I change my mind." Turn to **342**.

297

The knight is no easy opponent. Perhaps you should flee while you still can. (If you do, he will hit you for 1–6 Stamina points as you run off.)

Silent Knight, COMBAT 7, Defense 12, Stamina 7

If you run away	turn to **23**
If you win	turn to **320**

298

Tendrils of magical force hold you rooted to the spot. The corpse's bleak gaze burrows into your soul like a maggot into decaying flesh. To escape its clutches you must make a MAGIC roll at a Difficulty of 15.

Successful MAGIC roll	turn to **321**
Failed MAGIC roll	turn to **275**

299

The belfry contains nothing of interest. You decide to leave before the bats awaken and find you here. Hurrying back down the stairs, you return the way you came. Turn to **22**.

300

An elf approaches out of the foliage surrounding you. He looks like a green candle-flame against the darkness. In his hands he has a slim silver sword, which he presents to you with a solemn bow. "Now my debt to you is repaid," he murmurs before vanishing off into the depths of the wood.

You get a **silver sword (COMBAT +1)** but must lose the codeword *Bosky*.

Follow the elf	turn to **22**
Continue searching the woods	turn to **93**

301

The temple of Alvir and Valmir is a great pillared edifice of blazing white marble on the esplanade looking out over the bay. The twin gods are responsible for storms at sea. In the nave of the temple, a mural depicts them as fishers hauling up the souls of the drowned in their nets.

If an initiate	turn to **269**
If not an initiate	turn to **292**

302

Wishport market is located in a maze of alleys adjacent to the waterfront. Each alley is dedicated to a different commodity. In one you can buy rope, in another lanterns, and so on. You hear the echo of hammer on anvil from the weaponsmith's forge just ahead.

Armor	To buy	To sell
Leather (Defense +1)	50 Shards	45 Shards
Ring mail (Defense +2)	100 Shards	90 Shards
Chain mail (Defense +3)	200 Shards	180 Shards
Splint armor (Defense +4)	—	360 Shards
Plate armor (Defense +5)	—	720 Shards
Heavy plate (Defense +6)	—	1440 Shards

Weapons (sword, axe, etc)	To buy	To sell
Without COMBAT bonus	50 Shards	40 Shards
COMBAT bonus +1	250 Shards	200 Shards
COMBAT bonus +2	—	400 Shards
COMBAT bonus +3	—	800 Shards

Magical equipment	To buy	To sell
Amber wand (MAGIC +1)	—	400 Shards
Ebony wand (MAGIC +2)	—	800 Shards
Cobalt wand (MAGIC +3)	—	1600 Shards

Other items	To buy	To sell
Lockpicks (THIEVERY +1)	—	270 Shards
Holy symbol (SANCTITY +1)	200 Shards	100 Shards
Compass (SCOUTING +1)	500 Shards	450 Shards
Parchment	2 Shards	1 Shard
Rope	50 Shards	45 Shards
Lantern	100 Shards	90 Shards

Items which have no purchase price listed are not available locally.

The market is where you can buy and sell possessions to carry on your person. To buy trade goods that can be carried onboard a ship, you need to visit the warehouses at the waterfront.

When you're through here, turn to **217**.

THE ENCHANTED WATERFALL

303

You come to a pool at the bottom of a waterfall. Here a fine spray hangs in the air like sparkling mist. The longer you look at it, the more you imagine you can see dancing figures outlined in the mist. Above the roar of the waterfall you seem to hear soft voices calling out to you.

Stay here a while longer	turn to **692**
Leave now	turn to **716**

304

The road is built of old gray cobblestones, which are now half overgrown with a carpet of rich, green grass. Sometimes you

pass a patrol of soldiers or a peasant leading his cattle to market. You do not expect any trouble on this well-patrolled stretch of road.

Roll two dice for encounters:

Score 2-6	An eerie light in the dusk	turn to **34**
Score 7	An uneventful journey	turn to **11**
Score 8-12	A pardoner	turn to **691**

305

The Haunted Hills are virtually uninhabited, except for will-o'-the-wisps, monsters, and a few mad outcasts. Roll two dice to see what you encounter:

Score 2-4	A sulphurous cave	turn to **760**
Score 5-6	A prophet of doom	turn to **394**
Score 7	A trouble-free journey	turn to **172**
Score 8-9	Outlaws	turn to **419**
Score 10-12	A hungry ghost	turn to **444**

306

The countryside between the River Grimm and the Whistling Heath is dotted with quaint villages where the tavern talk is of elfin glades and the pranks of goblins at night. Roll two dice:

Score 2-4	An unusual wager	turn to **597**
Score 5-7	A night at an inn	turn to **621**
Score 8-9	An uneventful journey	turn to **153**
Score 10-12	A chuckling in the woods	turn to **645**

307

The ship weighs anchor and steers majestically out of Ringhorn harbor. "This'll be a trouble-free haul," thinks the captain. "I can smell it on the wind."

He is obviously a seasoned mariner. Fifteen days later you are putting into dock at Yellowport. On the way there has been no sign of pirate vessels and just a steady strong breeze to carry you on your way. If only every sea voyage could be so uneventful!

Turn to **140** in *The War-Torn Kingdom*.

308

You approach the captain of a Sokaran brigantine which is soon to set sail. He is happy to make a little extra money by taking a paying passenger along. You soon discover that passage to Marlock City or Ringhorn will cost you 10 Shards, while passage to Yellowport costs 15 Shards. You can pay the fare and set sail at once, or give up and review your other options instead.

Set sail for Yellowport	turn to **239**
Set sail for Marlock City	turn to **262**
Set sail for Ringhorn	turn to **163**
Don't put to sea yet	turn to **33**

309

The road winds its way past countless numbers of farms, passing through villages where the peasants live well on their bountiful harvests.

Roll two dice for encounters:

Score 2-5	A loathsome lady	turn to **475**
Score 6-7	An uneventful journey	turn to **35**
Score 8-12	A minstrel	turn to **500**

310

You are on the road leading from the Monastery of Molhern to Wheatfields, the market capital of central Golnir.

Go southeast to the monastery	turn to **94**
Head northwest to Wheatfields	turn to **333**
Head southwest to the Whistling Heath	turn to **195**
Head northeast to the Rainbow River	turn to **123**

311

The tavern costs you 1 Shard a day. Each day you spend here, you can recover 1 Stamina point if injured, up to the limit of your normal unwounded Stamina score. When you are ready to leave, turn to **2**.

312

An old hogwarden tells you that the Abbey of Lacuna lies to the north. "It's at the end of a winding road that only the faithful can ever find," he claims.

Go north	turn to **7**
Go south	turn to **168**
Go east	turn to **99**
Go west	turn to **237**

313

Each time you slice through one of the hydra's necks, it grows another head. You soon see that the only way to defeat it is to strike at the point where all the necks join the body.

Hydra, COMBAT 6, Defense 11, Stamina 9

If you kill it, turn to **361**.

314

You leave Castle Orlock behind. Roll two dice:

Score 2-6	Pursued	turn to **600**
Score 7	Uneventful journey	turn to **268**
Score 8-9	A pitfall	turn to **337**
Score 10-12	Smugglers	turn to **360**

315

Castle Ravayne is virtually a city in its own right: the outer courtyard is filled with stables, grain stores, pens for livestock, carpentry yards, and a blacksmith. Nearby, some knights are keeping fighting-fit by charging with lances at a straw-filled dummy. Beyond, another line of defenses encloses the inner keep.

Visit the shrine to the war-god Tyrnai	turn to **43**
Visit the armory	turn to **66**
Practice swordplay	turn to **89**
Rob the treasury	turn to **624**
Enter the inner keep	turn to **112**
Leave the castle	turn to **118**

316

Resurrection costs 200 Shards if you are an initiate, 600 Shards if not. (If you have the title *Chosen One of Nagil*, it is free of charge.)

Resurrection is the last word in insurance. Once you have arranged for resurrection you need not fear death, as you will be magically restored to life here at the temple.

To arrange resurrection, pay the fee and write *Temple of Nagil* (*Cities of Gold and Glory* **339**) in the Resurrection box on your Adventure Sheet. If you are later killed, turn to **339** in this book.

You can have only one resurrection arranged at a time. If you arrange another resurrection later at a different temple, the original one is canceled. (Cross it off your Adventure Sheet. You do not get a refund.)

When you are finished here, turn to **125**.

317

Becoming an initiate of Lacuna gives you the benefit of paying less for blessings and other services the temple can offer. It costs 30 Shards to become an initiate. You cannot do this if you are already an initiate of another temple.

If you choose to become an initiate, write *Lacuna* in the God box on your Adventure Sheet—and remember to cross off the 30 Shards. Once you have finished here, turn to **294**.

318

The high priestess sweeps forward and divests you of the three talismans. "What a thoughtful gift!" she trills. "The goddesses will be so pleased."

Cross the **four-leaf clover, silver horseshoe,** and **rabbit's foot charm** off your Adventure Sheet. Later, you are strolling across the village green when a huge gold nugget whistles down out of the sky and thuds into the grass right in front of you.

"That's handy, Harry," remarks a nearby alewife to her husband.

You sell the nugget for 999 Shards. After recording the money on your Adventure Sheet, turn to **81**.

319

You are given a sound thrashing for your impertinence. Lose 2 Stamina points and (if still alive) roll a die.

Score 1-3	Thrown in the dungeon	turn to **365**
Score 4-5	Thrown in the moat	turn to **118**
Score 6	Let off with a warning	turn to **315**

320

Your opponent falls with a hollow clatter to the ground, releasing a wisp of green vapor. When you throw open the visor, you are amazed to see the armor is empty.

The dwarf comes running out of the pavilion in a state of high anger. "You cheated!" he says. "It isn't fair. I will have my revenge." So saying, he darts off into the bushes.

Get the codeword *Baluster*. You can take the remnants of your uncanny opponent: **plate armor (Defense +5)** and a **jagged sword (COMBAT +1)**. Also roll two dice, and if the total is higher than your COMBAT score then increase it by 1.

| Continue along the path | turn to **343** |
| Leave the forest | turn to **23** |

321

Severing the spells that held you transfixed, you send forth a golden light that forces the vampire knight to recoil in pain. You lose no time in racing off, not stopping until you are out of the Forest of the Forsaken. Turn to **23**.

322

The more treasure you collect, the longer it will take and the greater the chance the bats will notice you. Decide how much you will collect, then roll two dice and add 1 to the total for every 100 Shards you have taken.

| Score 2-10 | You leave with your loot | turn to **345** |
| Score 11+ | The vampire bats awaken | turn to **368** |

323

The creature's armor is too heavy to suit you, but you can take a **hunting spear**, a **boar's tusk,** and the 30 Shards that it had in its purse. Record your acquisitions and then turn to **93**.

324

The temple of Elnir is a majestic palace of black marble inlaid with veins of gold. Elnir is the foremost god of the pantheon, the patron of warlords and kings. His realm is said to lie between the mountains and the sky, and whenever there is a storm the simple folk say, "Something has angered Elnir."

Become an initiate of Elnir	turn to **63**
Renounce his worship	turn to **86**
Seek a blessing	turn to **109**
Leave	turn to **2**

325

The harbor of Wishport. Here you can buy a ship, or put one to sea, if you already have a ship docked at this location. It is also possible to visit the warehouses lining the waterfront, where goods from afar are bought and sold in quantity.

Buy a ship	turn to **233**
Sell a ship	turn to **256**
Go aboard your ship	turn to **279**
Hire a crew for your ship	turn to **50**
Pay for passage on a ship	turn to **73**
Visit the warehouses	turn to **96**
Go to the city center	turn to **217**

326

These are eerie woods haunted by the rustling of leaves and the occasional mournful cry of an animal far off between the trees. Not many people are to be seen this far from the farmlands of the river valley. Roll two dice:

Score 2-4	Smoke over the treetops	turn to **620**
Score 5-6	A robber	turn to **644**
Score 7-8	Uneventful journey	turn to **349**
Score 9-12	A hole under an oak tree	turn to **668**

327

You are traveling on an old stone road. Carved limestone monoliths occur at intervals of seven leagues, each with an inscription marking the distance to the High King's Seat.

Roll two dice for encounters:

Score 2-7	Pilgrims	turn to **740**
Score 8-9	An uneventful journey	turn to **355**
Score 10-12	A plague-ridden hag	turn to **764**

328

The Endless Plains are called *The Breadbasket of Golnir*—a vast rolling expanse of fields that gleam in summer like quilts of gold. Pretty, whitewashed villages nestle beside lazy streams. The farms are filled with plump livestock. Danger is unknown to the inhabitants of this idyllic landscape.

When you are ready to head on toward fresh pastures, turn to **77**.

329

The road snakes on between the verdant farmland. To either side you see peasants working in the fields. The barns and thatched-roofed cottages present an idyll of peace and contentment.

Roll two dice for encounters:

Score 2-7	Seven fools	turn to **653**
Score 8-9	An uneventful journey	turn to **265**
Score 10-12	A mad thatcher	turn to **669**

330

You search through the taverns along the waterfront, looking for seasoned sailors willing to crew your vessel. It costs 20 Shards to upgrade a poor crew to average, 40 Shards to upgrade average to good, and 80 Shards to upgrade good to excellent. (These prices are cumulative, so the total cost of bringing a poor crew up to excellent is 140 Shards.) Once you've recorded any changes in the ship box on the back of your Adventure Sheet, turn to **255**.

331

Owning a ship has two advantages. First, it makes it much easier to travel around. Second, it allows you to get rich by trading goods in bulk. Goods are transported in Cargo Units. (A Cargo Unit weighs several tons—much more than one person could carry!)

The more expensive your ship, the greater its carrying capacity. More expensive ships are also more seaworthy.

Choose a ship from the types listed here.

Type	Cost	Capacity
Barque	250 Shards	1 Cargo Unit
Brigantine	450 Shards	2 Cargo Units
Galleon	900 Shards	3 Cargo Units

Record your ship in the Ship's Manifest. You get to choose the ship's name. The crew quality is average unless you hire on better sailors. Each time you arrive at a new destination, change the entry in the Docked column to the ship's current location. (So if you aren't going to sail right away, note that the ship is docked at Metriciens.)

Hire a better crew	turn to **354**
Leave the city	turn to **79**
Visit the warehouses	turn to **285**
Return to the city center	turn to **48**

332

A rugged track winds off through pasture land. A few rough looking types watch you askance as you pass them on the road.

Roll two dice for encounters:

Score 2-6	Devout priests	turn to **525**
Score 7-8	An uneventful journey	turn to **58**
Score 9-12	Coarse ruffians	turn to **550**

333

A tavern squats beside a millpond. Weeping willows shade the tables in the beer garden at the back. It looks like an inviting place to spend a few days.

Stop at the tavern	turn to **12**
Press onward	turn to **356**

334

Becoming an initiate of Sig gives you the benefit of paying less for blessings and other services. Also, you can add 1 to your THIEVERY score, as Sig will watch over your pilfering activities and keep you safe from the law. It costs 50 Shards to become an initiate. (You cannot do this twice to obtain a double THIEVERY bonus!) You cannot be an initiate of any other temple.

If you choose to become an initiate, write *Sig* in the God box on your Adventure Sheet—and remember to cross off the 50 Shards.

Once you have finished here, turn to **347**.

335

You are sailing in waters close to Port Ringhorn.

Go west	*The Court of Hidden Faces* **26**
Go south	*Over the Blood-Dark Sea* **200**
Go east	turn to **106**
Dock at Ringhorn	turn to **255**

336

Your arrival at the Abbey of Lacuna is greeted by friendly waves from the nuns. Hastening into the main building, you kneel to the abbess and tell her of your recent adventures.

"The goddess has guided you home to us," she says with a broad smile.

Seek a blessing	turn to **526**
Renounce initiate status	turn to **551**
Rest here for a while	turn to **576**
Leave at once	turn to **38**

337

Wily brigands have set a concealed trap out on the downs. To spot it in time to avoid getting caught, you need to make a SCOUTING roll at a Difficulty of 12.

Successful SCOUTING roll	turn to **268**
Failed SCOUTING roll	turn to **289**

338

The ground rises, becoming drier, and you realize you are leaving the Magwort Fens.

Go north	turn to **306**
Go west to Wishport	turn to **217**
Go east	turn to **130**

339

You are restored to life at the Temple of Nagil in Metriciens. Your Stamina is back to its normal score. The possessions and cash you were carrying at the time of your death are lost—cross them off your Adventure Sheet. Also remember to delete the entry in the Resurrection box now it has been used.

"Nagil be praised!" intone the priests. "Nagil is the greatest of all the gods."

Dazed by the experience of rebirth, you stumble outside for a breath of fresh air. Turn to **48**.

340

To renounce the worship of Lacuna, you must pass an ordeal of judgment. This entails the high priestess shooting a silver arrow at you along the length of the nave. "If Lacuna bears you no ill will, the arrow will miss its target," you are assured.

Submit to the ordeal	turn to **378**
Stay an initiate after all	turn to **294**

341

As a member of the nobility, you are admitted to the castle without delay. Peasants' carts are pushed aside by the sentries so that you may sweep majestically past. Turn to **315**.

342

The inner keep of the castle is a mighty fortress with walls several meters thick. Narrow windows admit golden shafts of sunlight into the gloomy hallway.

If you have the title *Paladin of Ravayne* you know these ancient halls well, and there is even a private chamber set aside for your use.

Visit your chamber (if a *Paladin*)	turn to **661**
Visit the chapel of the god Elnir	turn to **379**
Seek out the wizard Estragon	turn to **21**
Request an audience with the baroness	turn to **44**
Leave the keep	turn to **315**

343

The foliage around you is filled with eerie rustling noises. The trunks of the trees are black and twisted with age. Before long you come to a fork in the path.

Go left	turn to **366**
Go right	turn to **22**
Go back	turn to **23**

344

At the back of the knight's crypt you find a **green medallion**. When you are ready to leave, turn to **22**.

345

You hurry back down the stairs. Your courage deserves a greater reward than mere treasure. Roll two dice, and if the result is greater than your current Rank you gain a Rank. You also gain 1-6 Stamina points *permanently*—that is, increase your normal (unwounded) Stamina score by the roll of one die. Remember that going up a Rank increases your Defense.

Once you have made any necessary adjustments to your Adventure Sheet, turn to **22**.

346

A **severed head** lies on top of a tree stump. Its eyes are open and, moving closer, you are given a nasty shock when it suddenly speaks: "I have a favor to ask. Would you take me to the hut of the hermit Knocklar? He's always taking me out with him when he goes to cut wood and then leaving me behind." Having said its piece, the **severed head** falls silent and closes its eyes. Add it to your list of possessions if you wish, then turn to **116**.

347

The temple of Sig is a narrow high-gabled edifice close to the waterfront. By name, Sig is the patron deity of lovers, vagabonds, and traveling entertainers, but he is also god of cunning and deception, and as such is worshipped by those who live outside the law.

Become an initiate of Sig	turn to **334**
Renounce the worship of Sig	turn to **375**
Seek a blessing	turn to **13**
Leave	turn to **2**

348

You can leave possessions and money here to prevent having to carry them around with you. Record in the box anything you wish to leave. Each time you return, roll two dice:

Score 2-9	Your possessions are safe
Score 10	A thief; all the money you left here is gone
Score 11	A gang of burglars; lose all possessions you left here
Score 12	A fire; your town house and all its contents have been destroyed

You can also rest at your town house for as long as you wish. If injured, restore your Stamina to its normal unwounded score.

When you've finished at your town house, turn to **217** (and remember to erase the checkmark in the town house box if it was destroyed by fire).

```
Items at town house




```

349

You are journeying through sparsely inhabited country east of the Endless Plains. Northward lie the Haunted Hills. Somewhere off to the south is the town of Goldfall, where it is said that nuggets of precious metal drop each night from the sky.

Head west	turn to **328**
Go north	turn to **305**
Go south	turn to **123**
Go east	turn to **237**

350

The boat winds its way sluggishly upriver against the current. The rich fields gradually give way to grazing land and rugged heath. One evening at dusk you see a pallid green light flickering far off in the east, across the desolate countryside. The sailors tell you the light shines from the top of the Tower of Despair. "A haunted place where an ogre king once dwelt," adds the captain in a hushed voice.

The next day you arrive at Marmorek. This is as far as the boat is going. If you want to return south with them, you must pay another 5 Shards for your fare.

Stop off at Marmorek	turn to **167**
Sail back downriver	turn to **144**

351

You are traversing the Spine of Harkun mountain range. Distantly against the sky you can see the massive bulk of Sky Mountain. The forked snow-clad peak resembles a crone's broken tooth. According to legend, the moon once caught on the peak and the Mannekyn People had to fly up to break it loose. No human has ever scaled Sky Mountain, as far as you know.

Roll two dice for events along the way:

Score 2-6	A hydra	turn to **664**
Score 7-8	Nothing of note	turn to **640**
Score 9-12	Mannekyn People	turn to **688**

352

The road sweeps around through the meadows and fields of eastern Golnir. In places it is in dire need of repair. A peasant leaning on a turnstile tells you that a man once fell into one of the road's flooded potholes during the rainy season. " 'E wuz drowned!"

Roll two dice for encounters:

Score 2-6	The High King's messenger	turn to **693**
Score 7-8	An uneventful journey	turn to **310**
Score 9-12	The wizard Estragon	turn to **717**

353

You are on the coastal road. The great port city of Ringhorn lies not far to the west. The town of Metriciens is rather more distant to the east.

Head west	turn to **2**
Head east	turn to **373**
Leave the road and head north	turn to **78**

354

You trawl through the taverns along the waterfront, looking for able seamen willing to crew your vessel. It costs 15 Shards to upgrade a poor crew to average, and 30 Shards to upgrade average to good. You cannot upgrade higher than that in Metriciens, because there aren't enough good sailors.

Once you've recorded any changes in the ship box on the Ship's Manifest, turn to **33**.

355

You are on the ancient paved road between Delpton and Wheatfields.

Head west to Delpton	turn to **6**
Head east to Wheatfields	turn to **71**
Venture north over open country	turn to **52**
Strike out due south	turn to **75**

356

The sun is shining across the flower-filled meadows as you make your way from Tekshin's Tavern.

Take the road to Goldfall	turn to **332**
Take the road to Wheatfields	turn to **309**
Take the road to the Monastery of Molhern	turn to **352**
Go cross-country toward the Whistling Heath	turn to **195**

357

The merchants' guild in Ringhorn. Here you can bank your money for safekeeping—or invest it in guild enterprises in the hope of turning a profit. Acquire the codeword *Bastion* if you didn't have it already.

Make an investment	turn to **39**
Check on investments	turn to **62**
Deposit or withdraw money	turn to **36**
Return to the town center	turn to **2**

358

You are off the southern seaboard close to the wealthy mercantile city of Metriciens.

Go west	turn to **106**
Go south	*Over the Blood-Dark Sea* **301**
Go east	turn to **175**
Dock at Metriciens	turn to **33**

359

The broad, gently rolling pasturelands between the Grimm and the Rainbow Rivers lie before you. Wool is sent south from here to make the rich gowns of the merchant princes of Ringhorn and Metriciens. Roll two dice:

Score 2-6	Nuns from the Abbey of Lacuna	turn to **15**
Score 7-12	Uneventful journey	turn to **312**

360

You see a group of smugglers bringing their contraband ashore by the light of the moon.

Show yourself	turn to **415**
Continue on your way	turn to **268**

361

The hydra's bites were venomous. If it managed to injure you at all during the battle, turn to **377**. If not, turn to **17**.

362

Becoming an initiate of Nagil is not possible if you are already an initiate of another temple. You are made to undergo various trials to test your worthiness. In the last test, you are sealed in a casket below the ground and made to confront your own fears.

To pass the tests you must roll under your Rank on one die. If successful, write *Nagil* in the God box on your Adventure Sheet. Once you have finished here, turn to **257**.

363

If you are an initiate it costs only 10 Shards to purchase Lacuna's blessing. A non-initiate must pay 25 Shards.

Cross off the money and mark SCOUTING in the Blessings box on your Adventure Sheet. The blessing works by allowing you to try again when you make a failed SCOUTING roll. It is good for only *one* re-roll. When you use the blessing, cross it off your Adventure Sheet. You can have only one SCOUTING blessing at a time. Once it is used up, you can return to any branch of the temple of Lacuna to buy a new one.

When you are finished here, turn to **294**.

364

Sentries with huge black halberds block your way across the heavy drawbridge. To convince them to let you enter, you must make a CHARISMA roll at a Difficulty of 12.

Successful CHARISMA roll	turn to **315**
Failed CHARISMA roll	turn to **20**

365

There is only one thing to be said for the dungeon of Castle Ravayne: there aren't any rats. It's far too uncomfortable for rats.

Lose all your possessions and cash. Also lose the title *Paladin of Ravayne* if you had it.

If you have the codeword *Bashful*, turn to **430**. If not turn to **455**.

366

The path winds its way between steep earthen banks from which the roots of trees protrude like ossified snakes. It brings you to a squat crypt built of green-veined gray marble. Above the entrance rises a small pyramid with a stone eye carved into the summit. In the center of the eye sparkles an emerald as large as a duck's egg.

Climb up to get the emerald	turn to **91**
Enter the crypt	turn to **160**
Retrace your steps and take the other path	turn to **22**
Leave the forest	turn to **23**

367

The path leads to a clearing. In the middle stands a narrow windowless tower of jet black stone. Looking up, you see that the parapet of the tower is encrusted with small gems that glitter like stars. There is only a single door, banded solidly with panels of dark iron.

Turn to **138**.

368

Disturbed by the heavy chink of coins, a number of bats flutter down from the rafters and sink their fangs into your flesh. Roll one die. You must lose that many Stamina points *permanently*—i.e. reduce both your current and your normal (unwounded) Stamina score by this number. If you survive, you can shake off the bats and turn to **345**.

369

"Knocklar, you oaf!" says the severed head. "You dropped me in the forest again. If not for the kindness of this stranger I would be there until morning with beetles crawling up my nostrils!"

Knocklar takes the head and smiles at you. "You must stay a while and tell me of your adventures," he says. "I have renounced the world myself in favor of a life of spiritual contemplation."

"A life of drunken idleness, more like!" declares the head in outrage.

Knocklar leads you into his cottage where, ignoring the head's protests, he stuffs it into a breadbox. Then he invites you to stay and have supper with him.

Cross the **severed head** off your Adventure Sheet and then decide what you're doing now.

Stay for supper	turn to **481**
Ask Knocklar for a blessing	turn to **406**
Gossip with him	turn to **431**
Leave the hermitage	turn to **456**

370

From Ringhorn, you have the option to put to sea, travel upriver, or journey overland. The fare to travel upriver is 5 Shards.

To travel by sea, you must either possess a ship which is docked in the harbor (check the Ship's Manifest) or find a captain who is willing to take you as a passenger.

Go to the harbor	turn to **255**
Travel upriver (pay 5 Shards)	turn to **264**
Take the road north	turn to **26**
Take the coast road east	turn to **140**
Take the coast road west	*The Court of Hidden Faces* **150**

371

You are walking the riverbank beside the clear gurgling waters of the fast-flowing Rainbow River.

Head upstream	turn to **303**
Head cross-country to the west	turn to **30**
Head cross-country to the east	turn to **122**
Head downstream to Conflass	turn to **168**

372

This is wild windswept heathland where shepherds eke out a meager living.

Head toward the Haunted Hills	turn to **305**
Head toward the Forest of the Forsaken	turn to **7**
Follow the Rainbow River south	turn to **30**
Go east toward the River Grimm	turn to **53**
Go north up into the mountains	turn to **351**
Strike out westward	turn to **236**

373

At the side of the coastal road there is a weathered old fort. It looks abandoned, with moss covering the pitted black stones of its high walls. Its empty windows stare out to sea. It may be a relic from ancient times, when the ruthless Uttakin swept up out of the south to conquer all Harkuna.

Investigate the fort	turn to **9**
Head north over open country	turn to **78**
Take the road east	turn to **32**
Take the road west	turn to **140**
Go down to the beach	turn to **511**

374

You are on an ancient cobbled road. Wheatfields is not too far to the northeast. Far off to the southwest lies Castle Ravayne.

Head toward Wheatfields	turn to **71**
Head toward Castle Ravayne	turn to **120**
Leave the road and go west	turn to **75**
Leave the road and go east	turn to **98**

375

To renounce the worship of Sig, you must pay 50 Shards in compensation to the priesthood. "You will also lose the good will of the deity," the high priest warns you darkly.

Stay an initiate after all	turn to **347**
Pay 50 Shards and renounce your faith	turn to **59**

376

At last you locate a narrow winding path which leads to the Abbey of Lacuna. The moss-covered roofs of the abbey buildings loom above a hedge. As you approach the broad wooden gate, you see nuns in their green-and-brown robes working in the gardens. Turn to **61**.

377

You do not have long to celebrate your victory. The poison reaches your heart and you feel a stab of crippling pain. The only thing that can save you is a blessing of Immunity to Disease and Poison. If you have such a blessing, cross it off and turn to **17**. Otherwise you are dead within seconds.

378

You stand beside the door of the temple as the high priestess draws a bead on you with the sacred bow. The silver arrow glints menacingly in the afternoon sunlight. Then you hear the twang of the string as she shoots.

Roll two dice. If the total is higher than your Defense, the arrow finds its mark and you lose 1–6 Stamina points (roll a die to see how much). If the two dice score less than or equal to your Defense, the arrow misses.

Either way, if you survive then you are free to leave. Delete *Lacuna* from the God box on your Adventure Sheet and then turn to **294**.

379

Elnir's chapel is situated on an upper floor of the keep. As the guardian of rulership and law, he is the patron deity of the house of Ravayne.

Become an initiate of Elnir	turn to **67**
Renounce his worship	turn to **90**
Seek a blessing	turn to **113**
Leave	turn to **342**

380

You strike out from the path, forcing your way through the entangling undergrowth. Ferns sway off to one side, revealing a set of sparkling eyes in the gloom. Strange mutterings come from up in the branches. The eerie reputation of this forest is well deserved. Roll two dice:

Score 2-5	Elfin pranks	turn to **248**
Score 6-7	The denizens leave you alone	turn to **93**
Score 8-9	A voice calls out to you	turn to **47**
Score 10-12	Attacked by a wereboar	turn to **70**

381

Knocklar has plenty of chores to get done. "I must chop some firewood, feed my chickens, and go and check the traps out in the woods," he says. "So you'll pardon me if I don't stand around chatting with you all day."

Ask him for a blessing	turn to **406**
Request his advice	turn to **431**
Bid him farewell	turn to **456**

382

You reach a glade where a long table is laid out for a banquet. It is spread with silver plates piled high with succulent roast meat, spice cakes, warm fresh bread, and large ripe fruit. Carved oak chairs are set out for thirteen guests.

Sit and eat your fill	turn to **407**
Wait and watch	turn to **432**
Retrace your steps	turn to **22**

383

The seven fools are building a fence around a tree where a cuckoo is nesting. When you ask why, their explanation is that the song of the cuckoo tells them it is time to start sowing the crops. "If we keep the cuckoo penned up all year, we'll be able to get in two or even three harvests, won't we?"

Just as he says that, the cuckoo flies off.

The seven fools scratch their heads. "We'll have to build it higher next year," says one.

"Maybe we could get a grappling hook up on to a cloud," suggests another, but by this time you are sauntering away shaking your head. Turn to **265**.

384

Cross off all the money you are carrying. The brigands count it and give a sullen grunt. "Hardly worth collecting!" says one, spitting into the dust at his feet.

"I dunno," says the other. "After all, it's free money, isn't it?"

They dive into the woods bordering the road, leaving you to trudge on ruefully toward your destination. Turn to **353**.

385

You spend a restful night at the inn. If you are injured, recover 1 Stamina point. The innkeeper asks you to pay 1 Shard for the night's lodging, but he is a charitable man and will not insist if you are broke. When you are ready to set out, turn to **153**.

386

The approaching vessel at first seemed to be an innocent merchantman, but then your lookout points to the banks of oars. "A pirate galley!" he cries. Sure enough, at that moment the ship hoists the red pennant of the Kingdom of the Reavers. Her oars give her a good burst of speed over short distances, and she is soon bearing down on you.

Make a run for it	turn to **411**
Negotiate terms	turn to **436**
Fight it out	turn to **461**

387

Cross all money and possessions off your Adventure Sheet. You are lucky to have gotten away with your life. You hide inside a hollow tree until sunrise, but when you retrace your steps you cannot find the inn. Turn to **153**.

388

You continue on your way after promising you will inform the damsel's champion of her whereabouts. Get the codeword *Bridoon* and turn to **200**.

389

Frightened by the power of your magic, the three wizards offer tribute if you will release them from the curse. Roll one die to see what they offer you:

Score 1	a **scarab amulet**
Score 2	a **silver horseshoe**
Score 3	150 Shards
Score 4	a **gold and silver breastplate (Defense +4)**
Score 5	an **amber wand (MAGIC +1)**
Score 6	a **peacock feather**

As you won the duel, you also get a chance to increase your MAGIC score. Roll two dice, and if the total exceeds your MAGIC score, increase the score by 1.

When you have finished here, turn to **335**.

390

"I have neither the time nor the patience to teach you any more of my secrets," says Estragon. "Musty libraries and dingy laboratories are not the best places to seek knowledge in any case. Go out into the world; look around you. Nature is the book in which all mysteries are revealed."

He turns away, leaving you to find your own way back up to the castle.

Turn to **342**.

391 ❑

If the box above is empty, put a checkmark in it now and turn to **590**. If the box is marked and you have a **dragon's head**, turn to **614**. If the box is marked and you do not have a **dragon's head**, turn to **491**.

392

Sir Fontesque twirls his long mustache and demands the right of trial by combat. The next day you are obliged to meet him on the field in front of the keep. The truth of your accusation will be decided by the outcome of this duel, as ancient law dictates.

Sir Fontesque, COMBAT 7, Defense 13, Stamina 11

If you win, turn to **467**. If you surrender, turn to **319**.

393

Delpton market is small by the standards of the great cities of the south coast, but you may find some useful knickknacks. Items with no purchase price listed are not available locally.

Armor	To buy	To sell
Leather (Defense +1)	50 Shards	45 Shards
Ring mail (Defense +2)	100 Shards	90 Shards
Chain mail (Defense +3)	—	180 Shards

Weapons (sword, axe, etc)	To buy	To sell
Without COMBAT bonus	50 Shards	40 Shards
COMBAT bonus +1	250 Shards	200 Shards
COMBAT bonus +2	—	400 Shards

Other items	To buy	To sell
Compass (SCOUTING +1)	500 Shards	450 Shards
Rope	50 Shards	45 Shards
Lantern	100 Shards	90 Shards

When your business is finished here, turn to **6**.

394

An insane old man dressed in a long gray robe comes stumbling up the path toward you waving a stout stick. His spittle-streaked beard and wild mane of hair remind you of the temple images of Nagil, the Lord of the Departed.

"The world will soon end!" he cries. "What will it profit you then to have the goodwill of the gods? They are doomed just as we are, fool!"

He touches you with his stick and barges past, disappearing around a bend in the trail. When you hurry to catch up, you find he has vanished.

Lose any blessings or resurrection arrangements you had, then turn to **172**.

395

You find a tiny golden pebble worth 2 Shards. Although you return to town with a hangdog look, another prospector sees your find and is amazed. "It took me three weeks before I got my first sniff of gold!" he says. "You're a lucky devil, make no mistake."

Try again tomorrow	turn to **470**
Leave Goldfall	turn to **104**

396

Some say that the whistling wind carries secrets from the afterlife. Is it that or some sixth sense that tells you something important is going to happen?

Go north	turn to **496**
Go south	turn to **762**
Go east	turn to **521**
Go west	turn to **546**

397

You receive the blessing of Molhern. This allows you a second attempt at any one failed MAGIC roll. After the second roll (whether it is successful or not) the blessing is used up. Write: *MAGIC re-roll (one use)* under Blessings on your Adventure Sheet.

You cannot obtain a second blessing from Molhern until this one is used up.

Now turn to **28**.

398

The peddler has a few bargains among the bric-a-brac on his cart:

Item	To buy
Candle	1 Shard
Hunting spear	30 Shards
Leather armor (Defense +1)	50 Shards
Fishing hook	2 Shards
Parchment	2 Shards

After buying whatever you think might be useful, turn to **212**.

399

A heavy ship driven by churning paddles comes plowing its way through the waves toward your ship. "A slave ship from Uttaku!" gasps the captain. "Their vessel is powered by oxen, turning a shaft that moves those paddles. Tireless, but cumbersome and slow to maneuver. We might be able to outrun them."

Roll two dice:

Score 2-5	The slaver overhauls you	turn to **503**
Score 6-12	You get away	*The Court of Hidden Faces* **444**

400

Misshapen sprites with grotesque faces come scampering out of the hedge beside the road. Tittering to themselves, they prod you with gnarled fingers and discuss whether you are worth eating.

"Give us an emerald and we'll let you go," pipes up one of the sprites.

It seems they will accept a **green gem** to leave you in peace.

Give them a **green gem**	turn to **288**
Make a break for it	turn to **627**

401

"We've been on a diplomatic mission to Baroness Ravayne," says the leader of the Sokaran group. "She's promised sanctuary to our royal master if he should require it. Here, you must take this to him without delay."

You are handed a **coded missive**. Turn to **287**.

402

A cloud of plague spores rises up the moment you lift the lid. Choking, you retreat to the open. The spores are germinating inside your lungs. *Permanently* reduce your Stamina by 1–6 (the roll of one die) unless you have a blessing of Immunity to Disease and Poison. If you did have a blessing, remember it is now used up.

After amending your Adventure Sheet, turn to **716**.

403

As a hunter yourself, you doubt if the cats have reformed quite that readily. Catching a mouse, you fling it in among them and the congregation dissolves into the usual feline squabbling and cruelty.

With an angry oath, the stranger vanishes in a puff of brimstone smoke, leaving behind a diamond worth 300 Shards. Note this as cash on your Adventure Sheet, then turn to **153**.

404

You take three **swords**, a **candle,** and 75 Shards from the bodies before continuing on your way. Turn to **55**.

405

"I have a special boon for such a devout worshipper," says the god. He touches you on the brow, leaving a silvery mark in the shape of a skull. Note on your Adventure Sheet that you have the title *Chosen One of Nagil*.

Swirling darkness surrounds you. "Do not fear," you hear Nagil saying. "You are being returned to the vale of mortality."

Turn to **99**.

406

"Bless you!" he says, and indeed as he speaks those words you acquire the blessing of Immunity to Disease and Poison. Note this on your Adventure Sheet. It can be used *once* to negate the effect of disease or poison, and then you must cross it off.

"You can get more blessings like that from the temple of Maka," says Knocklar. "Tell them I sent you and you might get a discount. Now, if you'll excuse me...."

Turn to **456**.

407

Soon you are joined by a host of slender aristocratic figures in noble robes. You hardly noticed their arrival, nor do you quite manage to get a clear look at their faces. Someone beside you says something witty and you find yourself laughing. It is like being in a dream.

To wake up you must make a MAGIC roll at a Difficulty of 12.

Successful MAGIC roll	turn to **457**
Failed MAGIC roll	turn to **482**

408

The militiamen—a troop of twenty soldiers and a sergeant—go

tramping past with a jingling of chain mail. Their banner shows the black lion emblem of the House of Ravayne.

If you have a **severed head**, turn to **786**. If not, turn to **258**.

409

A troop of militiamen comes marching along the road. A knight wearing the black lion of Ravayne on his tabard and shield rides at the head of the column. If you have the codeword *Bullion*, turn to **588**. If not, turn to **353**.

410

The approaching vessel at first seemed to be an innocent merchantman, but then your lookout points to the banks of oars. "A pirate galley!" he cries. Sure enough, at that moment the ship hoists the red pennant of the Kingdom of the Reavers. Her oars give her a good burst of speed over short distances, and she is soon bearing down on you.

Make a run for it	turn to **435**
Negotiate terms	turn to **460**
Fight it out	turn to **485**

411

Roll two dice and add your Rank. (Subtract 1 from the total if you have a poor crew. Add 1 if you have a good crew. Add 2 if you have an excellent crew.)

Score 1-6	The pirates overtake you	turn to **461**
Score 7+	You outrun them	turn to **14**

412

The stranger leans closer, pressing his lips to your neck. You feel a pricking sensation. Jumping back, you see a trickle of blood on his sharp white teeth. A vampire!

Make a SANCTITY roll at a Difficulty of 12.

Successful SANCTITY roll	turn to **437**
Failed SANCTITY roll	turn to **462**

413

You break down the door of the tower and confront the evil knight who has imprisoned the damsel.

Evil Knight, COMBAT 4, Defense 5, Stamina 4

If you defeat him, you can set her free; get the codeword *Brisket* and turn to **200**.

414

Your curse is deflected by their countercharms. The encounter ends in a draw. Your sailors stand at the rail and shake their fists at the wizards as they sail away. "Those hell-spawned devils!" says the mate in a voice of strong emotion. "It's getting so as it's hardly safe to sail the regular shipping lanes."

Turn to **335**.

415

The smugglers stop rolling their barrels of whiskey up the beach and stare in amazement as you approach. Make a CHARISMA roll at a Difficulty of 12.

Successful CHARISMA roll	turn to **539**
Failed CHARISMA roll	turn to **564**

416 ❑

If the box above is empty, put a checkmark in it now and turn to **566**. If the box is marked and you have a **map of the mountains**, turn to **638**. If the box is marked and you do not have a **map of the mountains**, turn to **491**.

417

Sir Parpulax is of such obviously good character that everyone is prepared to vouch for him. He suggests that perhaps it is you who is the traitor. If you have the title *Paladin of Ravayne*, turn to **492**. If not, turn to **319**.

418

The innkeeper charges 1 Shard a day. This entitles you to a mat beside the common-room fire and two hot meals. Each day you spend here, you can recover 1 Stamina point if injured, up to the limit of your normal unwounded Stamina score. When you are ready to leave, turn to **443**.

419

You are ambushed by a band of outlaws in wolf-pelt jerkins. They jump up from behind a ridge. You see at a glance that they far outnumber you, but they make no move to attack. Their leader signals for his men to lower their crossbows before scrambling down from the ridge to speak with you. "No offense," he says with a grin, "but one lone wanderer isn't worth the trouble of robbing."

Maybe he'd think differently if he could see inside your money pouch? Or perhaps they are really put off because you look too tough to handle without casualties? See if you can impress them by making a THIEVERY roll and a CHARISMA roll, both at a Difficulty of 13.

Both rolls successful	turn to **494**
Fail one roll	turn to **519**
Fail both rolls	turn to **544**

420

You have almost given up hope when you dig up a speck of gold worth 2 Shards.

"What confounded luck!" says a nearby prospector. "That means there's a good chance of a large nugget being buried there somewhere."

You want to go on digging, but the daylight is going.

"I'll help you dig first thing tomorrow, if you like," says the prospector as you walk back to town.

Try again tomorrow	turn to **470**
Leave Goldfall	turn to **104**

421

The wind thunders across the heath, rattling a small heap of pebbles stacked up by other travelers to mark the way.

Go north	turn to **496**
Go south	turn to **521**
Go east	turn to **762**
Go west	turn to **546**

422

Your prayer is heard by Molhern, who responds by telling you to travel to far lands in search of lost knowledge. You resolve to set out for the coast at once to take ship for foreign parts. Turn to **74**.

423

You meet a youth who shamelessly confesses to all sorts of daring crimes. His stories give you some ideas of your own. Roll one die, and if you score higher than your THIEVERY you can increase it by 1. Then turn to **97**.

424

Three highwaymen rise up from the side of the road. Two carry swords, the third has a crossbow aimed at your chest. Their faces are masked, but you can tell from the steely glint of their eyes that these are dangerous men.

Hand over your money	turn to **746**
Fight	turn to **770**

425

You are sure someone is following you. Leading them around a pond, you lose them by ducking through a bank of fog. As you hurry away, you think you hear a snarl of frustrated rage. It makes you shudder—no human could have made that sound. Turn to **268**.

426

They take you aside and speak in hushed tones, even though the only person within earshot is a drunken peasant. "Can't be too careful," says one. "We're on a top-secret mission for General Marlock. Here, you'd better take him this."

You are handed a **coded missive**. Turn to **287**.

427

To your horror, the casket contains a moldered skeleton that comes to life as it feels the touch of fresh air. Grasping you by the throat, it drains some of your life force before vanishing with a peal of macabre laughter.

You stagger back. You have lost one Rank. This reduces your normal (unwounded) Stamina score by 1–6 and will also reduce your Defense by 1. After amending your Adventure Sheet, turn to **716**.

428

Scratching your head, you start to deliver your sermon, but the cats quickly get bored and wander off. "You don't have the knack," says the stranger. "You have to keep people's attention if you want to teach them the error of their ways." His tone is soothing, but he has a big triumphant grin on his face.

You have to give him all your possessions. (But not your money.) When you've done that, turn to **153**.

429

Your attempt to conjure an illusory dragon just produces a soft bang and a bad smell. Cackling with glee at your ineptitude, the witches cast an extraordinary hex on you. You now find that you are compelled to travel to the Haunted Hills without delay. You cannot stop at any towns or inns on the way. Once you reach the Haunted Hills, the compulsion will leave you and you can act normally. Now turn to **268**.

430

The traitor Sir Bredubar is in a cell nearby. He has not forgotten you, and bribes the jailer to poison your food. If you have a blessing of Immunity to Disease and Poison, cross it off and turn to **455**. Otherwise turn to **560**.

431

Knocklar scratches his chin. "I get to hear all sorts of bits and pieces," he says. "One tends to, if one keeps one's ears open. The only trouble is sorting the wheat from the chaff, so to speak."

Ask about the Tower of Despair	turn to **556**
Ask about the Watcher	turn to **531**
Ask about the four-leaf clover	turn to **506**
Ask about the dwarf at the pavilion	turn to **629**

432

You crouch down behind a bank of ferns to see what will transpire. Make a THIEVERY roll at a Difficulty of 12.

Successful THIEVERY roll	turn to **507**
Failed THIEVERY roll	turn to **532**

433

None of your men will agree to accompany you. Cursing them for their cowardice, you climb up to the strange ship's deck by means of a long ladder made of knotted human hair. No one is in sight. Furled, the huge sails hang like shrouds for burying dead giants. Sparkling mist swirls above the dark mahogany planks.

A single light shines through the gathering dusk. You investigate and find an open hatch, with steps leading down into the bowels of the ship. Drawn as if by magic, you descend until you reach a huge hold where grim silent figures wait to greet you. You sense you are not at sea any longer. You have strayed into the abode of the dead.

You won't see your ship and crew again. Cross them off the Ship's Manifest and then turn to **689**.

434

Thick black clouds pile up along the horizon.

If you have the blessing of Alvir and Valmir, which confers Safety from Storms, you can ignore the storm. Cross off your blessing and turn to **335**.

Otherwise the storm hits with full fury. Roll one die if your ship is a barque, two dice if it is a brigantine, or three dice if a galleon. Add 1 to the roll if you have a good crew; add 2 if you have an excellent crew.

Score 1-3	Ship sinks	turn to **459**
Score 4-5	The mast splits	turn to **534**
Score 6-20	You weather the storm	turn to **221**

435

Roll two dice and add your Rank. (Subtract 1 from the total if you have a poor crew. Add 1 if you have a good crew. Add 2 if you have an excellent crew.)

Score 1-6	The pirates overtake you	turn to **485**
Score 7+	You outrun them	turn to **335**

436

The pirates pull alongside and cast grappling hooks to seize your vessel. Within moments they are swarming aboard. You offer them your goods, but plead for the freedom of your crew. Make a CHARISMA roll at a Difficulty of 15.

Successful CHARISMA roll	turn to **510**
Failed CHARISMA roll	turn to **535**

437

You recite from the sacred scriptures. The vampire presses his hands to his ears, and runs to and fro issuing long terrible howls before finally escaping up the chimney. He leaves behind a **scarab amulet** and a **tarnished sword (COMBAT +1)**, which you can add to your possessions if you like.

You go back to bed. Turn to **385**.

438

He is so grateful that, after selling his goods at the market, he offers to put you up at his home for a few days. If you are injured, you can recover 2–12 Stamina points. (Roll two dice to see how many. Your Stamina cannot go above its normal unwounded score.) Now turn to **31**.

439

One of the sailors got so drunk on his first night ashore that he forgot to close the covers on the hold. You stumble over the edge in the darkness and fall, breaking your neck. (And it serves you right.) Turn to **560**.

440

Cross off the **candle** if you're using it, as it can be used only once. Exploring the castle, you find a library containing many dusty tomes. There is a tingle of sorcery in the stale air. If you want to read a book, roll two dice:

Score 2-5	turn to **529**
Score 6-8	turn to **554**
Score 9-12	turn to **579**

When you are ready to leave, turn to **314**.

441

"I desire you to go to Uttaku," says Vanna. "The Uttakin are said to be steeped in decadence. I am advised they no longer pose a military threat. See if this is true."

The audience is at an end. You bow and withdraw. Turn to **342**.

442

Sir Gargin secures a delay by promising he will give proof of his loyalty the next morning. During the night, an assassin creeps into the chamber where you are sleeping and attacks you with a knife.

You can flee from this fight, but then it will be assumed that your accusation against Sir Gargin was false, and you will lose the title *Paladin of Ravayne* if you have it.

Assassin, COMBAT 5, Defense 6, Stamina 5

If you flee	turn to **118**
If you win	turn to **517**

443 ❑

If the box above is empty, put a checkmark in it and turn to **468**. If it is already marked, turn to **6**.

444

The ghost of a man who died of starvation in these hills steals down on you in the night. It is barely visible as a gray film against the stars, and even though your eyes flicker open you take no notice. It waits till you roll over and go back to sleep, then creeps closer…

Make a SANCTITY roll at a Difficulty of 14 to see if your innate holiness keeps the ghost at bay until dawn.

Successful SANCTITY roll	turn to **172**
Failed SANCTITY roll	turn to **569**

445

You find nothing on your first day, but another prospector tells you that's not unusual.

"I reckon to hit a mother lode about once a month," he says. "That's enough to keep me satisfied."

He certainly seems to have very fine clothes—and you notice that, instead of digging himself, he employs a few common laborers to do the spade work.

Try again tomorrow	turn to **470**
Leave Goldfall	turn to **104**

446

The Whistling Heath is covered by the shadows of low clouds as they go flitting by, under the overcast glare of the sun.

Go north	turn to **762**
Go south	turn to **496**
Go east	turn to **521**
Go west	turn to **546**

447

The storyteller is sitting on a turnstile, regaling the children from a nearby village with his tales. Roll two dice:

Score 2-5	turn to **186**
Score 6-8	turn to **472**
Score 9-12	turn to **478**

448

The friar tells you that he recently passed through Goldfall. "People there imagine they will get rich by searching for gold that falls from the sky. But even if gold did fall from the sky each night, and there was enough for everyone in the world to collect a handful each morning, would that make you rich?"

He goes on his way. Turn to **235**.

449

These militiamen are employed by the mercantile guilds of Ringhorn and Metriciens to keep the roads safe. "If you're worried about thieves, you should invest in a town house and leave some of your money at home," advises the militia sergeant.

"Or better still, invest at the merchants' guild," suggests the captain.

Turn to **55**.

450

Three penniless wanderers tell you a tale of being washed up on a lonely shoreline. "Still, we're determined to make names for ourselves," they vow. Their predicament reminds you of your own early career, so you give them a tenth of any cash you have on you (rounding fractions up). Only later, while passing through a village, do you remember seeing their faces on a wanted poster. Turn to **288**.

451

The knight thanks you for your help. "Take my lance," he says. "I shan't need it against the churl who has my lady."

Note the **diamond lance (COMBAT +2)** on your Adventure Sheet. "It's a useful weapon to use against a hydra," calls back the knight as he rides off.

Lose the codeword *Bridoon* and turn to **31**.

452

It is a **magic sword (COMBAT +2)**. Record it on your Adventure Sheet. Before you can do anything else, you find the chamber is spinning around you. A dark vortex seems to open at your feet, and you plunge in. A few moments later you find yourself lying among the rushes at the river's edge. The waterfall is flowing again. The spirits have departed. Turn to **716**.

453

Disregarding the angry grumbling of the villagers, you draw water from the well and give it to the old woman. Gain 1 point of SANCTITY if you can roll higher than your current SANCTITY score on two dice. Unfortunately you also get the plague and must reduce your CHARISMA by 1—unless you have a blessing of Immunity to Disease and Poison. Make any necessary changes on your Adventure Sheet and turn to **355**.

454

The story concerns a hairy old bogle who used to eat anyone who strolled too close to his lair. One day he caught a young maid who begged to be given a day to set her affairs in order. This tickled the bogle's humor so much that he said he'd spare her life if she could tell him what his name was.

The maid pretended to go back home to see to her affairs, but in fact she hid near the bogle's lair. And she overheard him singing to himself:

"I'll be making a meal of a plump milkmaid
Who doesn't know my name is Friddle McCade!"

But, of course, when she came back the next day she *was* able to name the bogle, and so she lived happily ever after.

That seems to be the end of the story. Get the codeword *Bookworm* and turn to **235**.

455

You languish in the dungeon for months, gradually becoming weaker. The only food you are given is a slimy gruel filled with weevils. The water tastes like it comes straight out of the drains.

Unless you have a blessing of Immunity to Disease and Poison (in which case turn to **480** after crossing off the blessing), you soon succumb to fever. Roll two dice:

Score 2-5	You die	turn to **560**
Score 6-9	Lose 1-6 Stamina *permanently*	turn to **505**
Score 10-12	A miraculous recovery	turn to **480**

456

Knocklar takes you back to the trail since he's going in that direction himself. "My advice to you is never to stray off a path if you want to avoid trouble," he says.

On the way he pauses at one of his traps, where he is delighted to discover a rabbit. "That'll make a nice stew for me and Edmund tonight," he says. In a moment of whimsy he slices off one of its paws and threads it on a leather thong. "Here, this might bring you luck."

He hands you a **rabbit's foot charm** then bids you farewell. Turn to **22**.

457

You find yourself lying on a carpet of rustling leaves. Sitting up with a wince, you look around the glade. In place of the banqueting table there is just a fallen tree trunk. There are no high-backed chairs, only a ring of toadstools. Where you thought there had been a group of fur-robed lords and ladies, there are only several watchful owls sitting on a high branch.

You were nearly trapped by the elves' glamour. Luckily you shrugged off their spell in time. Roll two dice, and if the total is higher than your MAGIC score then you gain 1 point of MAGIC. Once you have done that, you can return along the path. Turn to **22**.

458

You are bundled in irons, divested of all your possessions and cash (cross them off) and hauled off to Castle Ravayne, where you are flung into the dungeons. Turn to **365**.

459

Your ship, crew, and cargo are lost. Cross them off the Ship's Manifest. The waves close over your head and your only thought now is to save yourself. Roll two dice. If the score is greater than your Rank, you are drowned. If the score is less than or equal to your Rank, you are swept miraculously toward the shore. Lose 1–6 Stamina points and (if you can survive that) turn to **559**.

460

The pirates pull alongside and cast grappling hooks to seize your vessel. Within moments they are swarming aboard. You offer them your goods, but plead for the freedom of your crew. Make a CHARISMA roll at a Difficulty of 15.

Successful CHARISMA roll	turn to **510**
Failed CHARISMA roll	turn to **535**

461

The pirate vessel crunches into the side of your ship. The attackers swarm aboard, screaming the war cry that has struck terror into many brave hearts over the centuries. Your men square off grimly with hooks, belaying pins, and anything else that comes to hand. They will die fighting rather than be enslaved.

Roll three dice if you are a Warrior, or two dice if you belong to any other profession. Add your Rank to this roll. Then, if your crew is poor quality, subtract 2 from the total. If the crew is good, add 2. If the crew is excellent, add 3.

Score 0-4	Calamity; you are killed	turn to **560**
Score 5-9	Crushing defeat; lose 2-12 Stamina	turn to **535**
Score 10-13	Forced to give in; lose 1-6 Stamina	turn to **510**
Score 14-17	The pirates withdraw	turn to **14**
Score 18+	Outright victory	turn to **536**

462

You must fight the vampire without the benefit of armor or weaponry.

Vampire, COMBAT 7, Defense 9, Stamina 14

It's too late to flee now. If you defeat the vampire, he turns into a gray mist and you can have his **scarab amulet** and **tarnished sword (COMBAT +1)**. Then turn to **385.**

463

The approaching vessel at first seemed to be an innocent merchantman, but then your lookout points to the banks of oars. "A pirate galley!" he cries. Sure enough, at that moment the ship hoists the red pennant of the Kingdom of the Reavers. Her oars give her a good burst of speed over short distances, and she is soon bearing down on you.

Make a run for it	turn to **488**
Negotiate terms	turn to **513**
Fight it out	turn to **538**

464

There is a defiant squeal and a warthog comes squelching through the rushes toward you. A very big warthog.

Warthog, COMBAT 5, Defense 6, Stamina 7

If you kill it, turn to **338.**

465 ❑

Roll two dice, and if you get higher than your SCOUTING score you can add 1 to it. If the box above is empty, put a checkmark in it and turn to **489**. If it was marked already, turn to **514**.

466

The Baroness listens with interest to your report. "It seems incredible that a race that was once feared for its martial prowess should now have sunk to such a level," she says. "It is an object lesson for us all."

Roll two dice, and if the total is higher than your THIEVERY score then increase it by 1. Vanna also orders her steward to pay you 100 Shards out of the castle treasury.

Lose the codeword *Element* and turn to **342**.

467

After the duel, the wizard Estragon leads you aside. "You were proved right according to the old ways," he says, "but no one really believes that Fontesque is untrustworthy. I'd advise you to leave and not show your face around here for a while."

Turn to **118**.

468

A merchant is packing to leave at the same time that you are. "You travel through Castle Ravayne quite a bit, I suppose?" he says. "We can expect a change there quite soon, I hear."

"What sort of change?"

"A new head of the House of Ravayne. The Knight of the Long Knife is plotting against that young sprat Vanna. Not that I care one way or the other. Merchants may be no better than thieves, as people say, but in that case the nobility are even worse—they're thugs!"

Get the codeword *Bobbin* if you do not have it. If you already have it, get the codeword *Bisect* as well. Then turn to **6**.

469

A long serpentine shape emerges from the cave, unfolds its wings like sheets of bronze, and flies at you spitting fire.

Dragon, COMBAT 9, Defense 11, Stamina 20

No retreat or surrender is possible. If you win, you can take the **dragon's head** as a trophy, then turn to **172**.

470

You go out the next day, and the next. Sometimes you find a tiny bit of gold. More often you come back to town empty-handed, and each day you swear that unless you strike it rich the next day you are going to give up looking. But it is too late—you have gold fever. You spend all your money on gadgets that are supposed to help with prospecting: copper sieves, dowsing rods, gold-sensitive ferrets, and so on. After six weeks you have nothing to show for it. You are flat broke, and the gadgets you bought are worse than useless. Sourly, you pack up and leave town, vowing never to return. Turn to **104**.

471

You sit down to rest on an old tree stump. Water has collected in a hollow in the side. Idly delving into the puddle, your fingers touch a hard metal object. You clean off the muck and find that you now have a **key of stars**.

Go east	turn to **94**
Go west	turn to **193**
Go south	turn to **54**
Go north	turn to **195**

472

He tells a story of a kindly old wizard who found a little dwarf asleep under a bush. He took the dwarf as his apprentice, but after only a month he woke up to find that the dwarf had stolen a suit of magic armor. This armor was empty but could still move and fight, because it contained an elfin ghost.

"As long as the visor was never opened, the ghost could not escape, and it had to do whatever the dwarf wanted...." the storyteller says to the children.

The day is wearing on, and it is time you were on your way. Get the codeword *Beltane* and turn to **374**.

473

The storyteller is sitting on a grassy knoll beside a leafy lane, regaling the children from a nearby village with his tales. Roll two dice:

Score 2–6	turn to **454**
Score 7–12	turn to **667**

474

The sun is sinking behind a shelf of cloud when you come across an ancient burial mound. Ghostly light flickers around the stone arch leading inside.

Enter the mound	turn to **578**
Press on	turn to **222**

475

A woman of remarkable ugliness is sitting by the side of the road. Most people cross over to the other side to avoid her, and a few children stop to pelt her with clods of earth until you shoo them away.

"Thank you," she says. "All I want now is a great big kiss." She has a face like a frog that's been hit with a hammer!

Give her a kiss	turn to **651**
Continue on your way	turn to **35**

476

He is outraged that you rescued his lady love. "That was my own sworn task, you varlet!" he cries, charging at you with raised mace.

Angry Knight, COMBAT 5, Defense 9, Stamina 6

If you win, you can take his **mace**, **diamond lance (COMBAT +2)**, and **chain mail (Defense +3)**. Then lose the codeword *Brisket* and turn to **31**.

477

It is a **magic shield (Defense +10)**. Record it on your Adventure Sheet.

Before you can do anything else, you find the chamber is spinning around you. A dark vortex seems to open at your feet, and you plunge in. A few moments later you find yourself lying among the rushes at the river's edge. The waterfall is flowing again. The spirits have departed.

Turn to **716**.

478

He tells a story of a trau that for some reason took up residence in a farmer's field. It caused no trouble until harvesttime, when it decided to make its bed in the haystacks. Each day the farmer and his sons piled up the bales of hay, only to find them scattered all over the field by the following morning.

"You know what that farmer did?" says the storyteller. "He got a pot of fairy mead, which the trau love. The trau got drunk on the mead that was left out for it, fell into a doze, and the farmer's sons killed it with their pitchforks when they found it the next day asleep in a haystack."

"Where did he get the fairy mead?" you ask.

"Ah. That's a different story."

Turn to **374**.

479

"You won't be eating me today, Friddle McCade," you tell him.

He's so astounded to hear you use his true name that his fetid mouth gapes open and he cannot make any reply as you saunter off. Turn to **153**.

480

If you are 5th rank or higher, turn to **530**. If you are 4th Rank or lower, turn to **555**.

481

You have a fine supper of roast turnips, leeks, and venison pie washed down with some cups of fairy mead. "The elves provide me with this mead," says Knocklar blearily, stabbing at the fire with a poker.

"That's uncommonly generous of them," you remark.

Knocklar gives a gleeful titter. "Generous my foot! If they don't provide it, I threaten them that I'll walk in among their revels at night and disrupt all the fun. They can't stand the odor of sanctity you see."

You sleep soundly and can recover 1–6 Stamina points (the score of one die) if wounded. Then next morning you hear Knocklar already up chopping wood. Turn to **381**.

482

The elves have snared you with their glamour. You are locked inside a waking dream. Even resurrection cannot save you—you will not die—you will merely spend an eternity in feverish fairy revelry, gradually fading out of the waking world until you are no more real than a shadow at midnight.

483

You talk fast and think faster. "This is the head of my poor brother," you say, falling to your knees in the roadway and sobbing. "He was captured by an ogre who cooked him—all except for the head, which the vile monster considered inedible. Now I am taking him to Castle Ravayne to plead with the wizard Estragon to restore him to life."

"It's not Estragon you want," says the sergeant. "Speak to the high priest of Tyrnai. He can intercede with the god to get people brought back to life."

"When he's sober," adds one of the troopers quietly.

Turn to **258**.

484

Thick black clouds pile up along the horizon. If you have the blessing of Alvir and Valmir, which confers Safety from Storms, you can ignore the storm. Cross off your blessing and turn to **358**.

Otherwise the storm hits with full fury. Roll one die if your ship is a barque, two dice if it is a brigantine, or three dice if a galleon. Add 1 to the roll if you have a good crew; add 2 if you have an excellent crew.

Score 1-3	Ship sinks	turn to **459**
Score 4-5	The mast splits	turn to **534**
Score 6-20	You weather the storm	turn to **198**

485

The pirate vessel crunches into your ship's side and the pirates swarm aboard, screaming their terrifying war cry. Your men square off grimly with hooks and belaying pins. They will die fighting rather than be enslaved.

Roll three dice if you are a Warrior, or two dice if you belong to any other profession. Add your Rank to this roll. If your crew is poor quality, subtract 2 from the total. If the crew is good, add 2. If the crew is excellent, add 3.

Score 0-4	Calamity; you are killed	turn to **560**
Score 5-9	Crushing defeat; lose 2-12 Stamina	turn to **535**
Score 10-13	Forced to give in; lose 1-6 Stamina	turn to **510**
Score 14-17	The pirates withdraw	turn to **335**
Score 18+	Outright victory	turn to **584**

486

You hear the strains of bagpipe music. You sit on a milestone and listen for a while, but just as you are about to set off and look for the piper, the music stops. Turn to **222**.

487

Tekshin tells everyone that he lost his wings while serving in the Sokaran army. He is anxious that the truth should not get out, as that would make him a laughing stock. He says you can stay at the inn free for as long as you like. Restore your Stamina to its normal unwounded score, then turn to **356**.

488

Roll two dice and add your Rank. Add 1 to the total if you have an average crew, 2 if you have a good crew, or 3 if you have an excellent crew.

Score 1-6	The pirates overtake you	turn to **538**
Score 7+	You outrun them	turn to **221**

489

In the middle of the fens there is an island hemmed in by bulrushes. On this island you find a chest decorated with intricate mother-of-pearl inlays. Lifting the lid, you find a **golden katana (COMBAT +1).** You then retrace the treacherous path through the mire. Turn to **338**.

490

"I require a scarab amulet for one of my experiments," says Estragon. "Go and find one. When you bring it here I'll reward you well."

Turn to **342**.

491

You wait in a long line of courtiers who are being presented to Vanna. When it is your turn, she gives you a look of palpable displeasure, saying only a few curt words before passing on to the next person.

"How have I displeased the baroness?" you ask Sir Debrumas as he shows you out.

"Return with better tidings next time you come," is all he will say. Turn to **315**.

492

"I cannot allow my knights to slander one another," says Vanna in stern outrage. "Such a thing only fosters discontent. I will not have my realm eaten away from within, like a bad apple!"

Too late, you remember that Parpulax is her uncle. You are stripped of the title *Paladin of Ravayne*. Cross it off your Adventure Sheet and turn to **315**.

493

You will not find much of interest in the stores at Marmorek. "Pick-axes, candles, tents, buckets, sieves—all you need for mining and prospecting, friend!" declares the store owner jovially.

Armor	To buy	To sell
Leather (Defense +1)	50 Shards	45 Shards
Ring mail (Defense +2)	—	90 Shards

Other items	To buy	To sell
Pick-axe	50 Shards	40 Shards
Compass (Scouting +1)	500 Shards	450 Shards
Rope	50 Shards	45 Shards
Lantern	100 Shards	90 Shards
Parchment	2 Shards	1 Shard
Candle	5 Shards	4 Shards
Tent	150 Shards	135 Shards

Items with no purchase price listed are not available locally. When you're through here, turn to **190**.

494

"You're a man after my own heart," you tell the outlaw leader. He soon sees from your tales of skulduggery and daring adventure that you are in a higher league than his motley band of men. The outlaws ask you to stay and lead them for a while.

Accept the offer	turn to **72**
Refuse	turn to **519**

495

The trau come burrowing straight up out of the ground, leaving piles of soil like huge molehills. Rushing around, fluttering like busy black moths in the moonlight, they quickly erect stalls with luminous silk awnings. Then they look at you with wide grins and invite you to trade.

Note that the trau do not accept Shards. You must use the odd onyx coins called Mithrals if you wish to do business with them.

Armor	To buy	To sell
Vulcanium mail		
(Defense +7)	1600 Mithrals	1000 Mithrals
Weapons (sword, axe, etc)	To buy	To sell
COMBAT bonus +3	900 Mithrals	600 Mithrals
COMBAT bonus +4	1200 Mithrals	900 Mithrals
Magical equipment	To buy	To sell
Cobalt wand		
(Magic +3)	1800 Mithrals	1200 Mithrals
Selenium wand		
(Magic +4)	2000 Mithrals	1333 Mithrals
Other items	To buy	To sell
Fairy mead	1000 Mithrals	900 Mithrals
Four-leaf clover	25 Mithrals	20 Mithrals
Boar's tusk	20 Mithrals	15 Mithrals

When you have finished your business with the Trau, turn to **545**.

496

Goblins pelt you with stones from the top of a nearby peak. Roll two dice and subtract your armor's Defense bonus (if any). The result is how many Stamina points you lose.

Go east	turn to **94**
Go west	turn to **193**
Go south	turn to **54**
Go north	turn to **195**

497

A metal automaton with a goat-like head clanks forward to attack you. You parry its first few blows, but you soon realize that it is tireless and unkillable. Turning to flee, you are struck heavily across the shoulders. Roll two dice and subtract your armor's Defense bonus (if any) from the roll. The result is how many Stamina points you lose. If you survive, turn to **373**.

498

The gypsies offer to sell you a **rabbit's foot charm** for 30 Shards. "It'll bring you good luck, friend," insists a grinning old woman with a face like a walnut.

Buy the **rabbit's foot charm** if you wish, then turn to **371**.

499

You stumble upon thirteen witches dancing in a circle of old standing stones. They are livid at your intrusion, and challenge you to a contest of sorcery. You see no way to back out without antagonizing them even more. Make a MAGIC roll at a Difficulty of 11 to convince them to let you go on your way unmolested.

Successful MAGIC roll	turn to **268**
Failed MAGIC roll	turn to **429**

500

You pass through a village. A minstrel is standing on the village green singing a song:

"I crept into a ruined castle,
Then ran away, by golly.
And how I nearly suffered
For my greed and my folly!
Something followed me, you see,
Across the windswept heather,
And it would've caught me, too,
If I hadn't used a feather!"

You cannot be bothered to listen to any more of this awful doggerel. Turn to **35**.

501

The bogle picks you up and is about to pop you in his mouth. His breath makes an open drain smell as sweet as a bouquet of flowers, and his teeth look like jagged bits of flint. You had better think fast if you don't want to end up being picked out of those teeth with a bit of matchwood.

Make a CHARISMA roll at a Difficulty of 10.

Successful CHARISMA roll	turn to **504**
Failed CHARISMA roll	turn to **560**

502

You help yourself to a stack of gems and jewelry worth 900 Shards. Note this as cash on your Adventure Sheet.

Now comes the difficult part. You have to sneak past the guards outside without them spotting you. Carrying all this loot, it won't be easy. Make a THIEVERY roll at a Difficulty

of 16.

Successful THIEVERY roll	turn to **552**
Failed THIEVERY roll	turn to **577**

503

The slavers' vessel crunches into the side of your ship. As the attackers swarm aboard, your men prepare to defend themselves with whatever comes to hand.

Roll two dice:

Score 2–4	Calamity; you are killed	turn to **560**
Score 5–9	Crushing defeat; lose 2–12 Stamina	turn to **528**
Score 10–12	The slavers retreat	*The Court of Hidden Faces* **444**

504

"I hope this won't spoil your appetite," you say to the bogle.

He squints at you. "Spoil my appetite for what?"

"For those seven lovely plump milkmaids I saw coming along the path a bit behind me."

He licks his lips. Either that or he's halfway through eating a giant eel. "Mmmm, I love milkmaids," he says. "Very tasty. But you're right that I couldn't manage seven of them after eating you. Decent of you to tell me."

"No problem. I'll just wait over here, and you can eat me later."

A sudden glint of suspicion appears in his beady little eyes, but by that time you are running away for all you're worth. It's a good thing bogles are so stupid. Turn to **153**.

505

You lapse into a coma. Taken for dead, you are flung out on to the rubbish heap beyond the castle walls. Slowly your will to survive asserts itself and you crawl away to the river, where you drink deeply before curling up to sleep in the reeds.

Turn to **118**.

506

"You can get it off the trau," says Knocklar. "They love to collect the stuff for some reason."

"All very well, but where can I find the trau?" you ask him.

"Try Haggart's Corner. They sometimes show up there."

Turn to **456**.

507

You watch the elves of the Forsaken Forest come slinking out of the shadows. Their faces are narrow and fox-like, their bodies slim as saplings. A few are wrapped in rich furs. The others go naked.

They sit and eat, but their revelry is muted. Every now and

then, one of them will look around suspiciously and murmur: "But I could swear the air has a mortal smell …"

Eventually they melt away into the woods again. You take the opportunity to pilfer a jug of **fairy mead** from their banqueting table before heading back down the path. Turn to **22**.

508

A golden plaque is embedded in the rock face here. You clean away the grime with your finger, hoping to find an interesting message, but it seems to be gibberish: *VJ AM LAP AS PCX IS WSAQMM OV JAS PHI V LIV JAM GVAQV JUD JT AV JAH SPUD JT VIV LAV JET JMF*

Perhaps it is an inscription in the language of Old Uttaku? Or is it some sort of cipher?

Climbing back down, you continue on your way. Turn to **533**.

509

Thick black clouds pile up along the horizon.

If you have the blessing of Alvir and Valmir, which confers Safety from Storms, you can ignore the storm. Cross off your blessing and turn to **14**.

Otherwise the storm hits with full fury. Roll one die if your ship is a barque, two dice if it is a brigantine, or three dice if a galleon. Add 1 to the roll if you have a good crew; add 2 if you have an excellent crew.

Score 1-3	Ship sinks	turn to **459**
Score 4-5	The mast splits	turn to **534**
Score 6-20	You weather the storm	turn to **14**

510

The pirates take your cargo, all your possessions, and your cash. They also seize your ship for themselves (assuming it was your own ship in the first place). Cross all these off the Ship's Manifest. The pirates are convinced it is worth leaving you alive, at least. "Yes, that way we can prey on you again in the future," says their leader with a feral grin. "Every good fisherman knows to throw some of his catch back!"

You are put off in Metriciens. As the pirates sail off, you vow revenge. Turn to **48**.

511

You descend the cliff path to a stretch of beach. A fishing village is set at the top of the beach—small stone houses with slate roofs. Nets and boats lie on the pebbles in front of a groyne. As you approach, a couple of fishermen look up and wave.

Talk to them	turn to **561**
Walk along the beach	turn to **585**
Return to the top of the cliffs	turn to **373**

512

Write *Nagil* in the God box on your Adventure Sheet. (If you were already an initiate of another god, you now lose that status, as you cannot be an initiate of more than one god at a time.)

"Now you can arrange resurrection," the knights tell you. "Just go to any temple of our sweet lord Nagil."

So saying, they ride off. Turn to **127**.

513

The pirates pull alongside and cast grappling hooks to seize your vessel. Within moments they are swarming aboard. You offer them your goods, but plead for the freedom of your crew. Make a CHARISMA roll at a Difficulty of 15.

Successful CHARISMA roll	turn to **510**
Failed CHARISMA roll	turn to **535**

514

A knight in Samurai armor is sitting beside the empty chest. Seeing you, he looks up and says: "So, villain, you return to the scene of your crime!"

Samurai, COMBAT 6, Defense 12, Stamina 7

If you kill him, you can take his **splint armor (Defense +4)** and **ivory-handled katana**. Then turn to **338**.

515

"Excellent!" says Estragon, snatching the **scarab amulet** eagerly from your hands.

He teaches you a few simple enchantments. Roll two dice, and if the total is higher than your MAGIC score you gain 1 point of MAGIC.

Remember to cross the **scarab amulet** off your Adventure Sheet, then turn to **342**.

516

"I have heard many stories of a strange land called Akatsurai," says the baroness. "Travel to this land and seek out its ruler. Convey my best wishes to him or her, and inquire whether a legate may be sent to in order to strengthen diplomatic and trading links."

With that, she gives an imperious wave and Sir Debrumas escorts you out. Turn to **342**.

517

You can take the **assassin's dagger**. Faced with the dead body on the morrow, Sir Gargin admits he employed the fellow, but claims he was just supposed to give you a warning.

Vanna cannot decide who is telling the truth. She commands you both to leave the castle for a while until tempers have cooled. Turn to **118**.

518

Colossal limestone crags tower on all sides.

Go west	*The Court of Hidden Faces* **159**
Go east	turn to **351**
Go south	turn to **259**
Go north	*The Plains of Howling Darkness* **100**

519

After a friendly chat around their campfire, you settle down with the outlaws overnight and make ready to travel on the next morning. You can recover 1 Stamina point if injured.

It is only after you have gone several miles that you think to look in your belt-pouch. You find that all your money is there—no, not all of it. One single Shard has been taken.

You smile and close the pouch. People say there is no honor among thieves, but you *know* there is certainly pride. Turn to **172**.

520

You go out to the circle of standing stones and wait. The sun sinks slowly into the west, leaving a lilac sky waiting for the coming of night. There is a warm scent of honeysuckle on the breeze. Roll two dice:

Score 2-5	The trau arrive	turn to **495**
Score 6-12	A fruitless vigil ends at dawn	turn to **173**

521

You stop for a rest and doze off. When you are ready to set out on your travels again, you are disgusted to discover that while you were sleeping an invisible thief stole 1–6 of your possessions. (Roll a die to find how many. Possessions are stolen in the order they were written down on your Adventure Sheet.)

Go east	turn to **496**
Go west	turn to **595**
Go south	turn to **124**
Go north	turn to **546**

522

A blast of heat erupts from behind the door, burning away your hair and blistering your skin in seconds. Slamming the door shut, you stagger back outside.

Lose 1–6 Stamina points *permanently*—i.e. reduce both your current and unwounded Stamina by the roll of one die. In addition, you lose 1 point of CHARISMA because of the disfiguring burns.

If you are still alive, turn to **373**.

523

The fishermen are in a quandary. They cannot go home to their wives until they have caught some fish, but they have lost their only hook. "Can you help?" they implore.

Give them a **fishing hook** (if you have one)	turn to **631**
Tell them you can't help	turn to **371**

524

The merchants have plenty of goods to trade. Items without a buying price listed are not stocked, but you can still sell such a thing if you have it.

Armor	To buy	To sell
Leather (Defense +1)	45 Shards	45 Shards
Ring mail (Defense +2)	95 Shards	90 Shards
Chain mail (Defense +3)	—	180 Shards

Weapons (sword, axe, etc)	To buy	To sell
Without COMBAT bonus	40 Shards	35 Shards
COMBAT bonus +1	—	180 Shards

Other items	To buy	To sell
Amber wand (MAGIC +1)	—	400 Shards
Lockpicks (THIEVERY +1)	300 Shards	270 Shards
Compass (SCOUTING +1)	500 Shards	450 Shards
Parchment	2 Shards	1 Shard

After finishing your business with the merchants, turn to **287**.

525

Five elderly priests in long robes are walking down the lane just ahead. Catching up, you ask them where they are bound.

"We travel all over Golnir," says the oldest, "teaching people about the gods."

"You must have met some strange sorts in your time."

He nods. "Indeed. The most intractable were the bald folk of the Forsaken Forest. They attack and murder anyone who has a head of hair, scalping them to make wigs."

"And do not forget the citizens of Dweomer," chimes in the youngest priest, a fellow of about sixty. "They admire godlessness as if it were a virtue."

Turn to **58**.

526

The blessing of Lacuna allows you to re-roll any failed SCOUTING attempt *once*. When you want to use the blessing, cross it off your Adventure Sheet and make a second try at the roll.

You can only have one blessing for each ability at any one time. Once your SCOUTING blessing is used up, you can return to the abbey for a new one.

Now turn to **576**.

527

You carelessly set off an alarm in the form of a large gold-plated gong molded into a solar face. It must be one of the miraculous creations of the wizard Estragon, because it is banging itself loudly and shouting "Intruder!" in a tinny voice.

The sentries come running. You are hauled off to the dungeon in chains. Turn to **365**.

528

"This one will make a fine slave!" says a burly Uttakin warrior, holding your half-conscious form up by the hair.

You are chained and herded below decks for the arduous haul back to Aku. Turn to *The Court of Hidden Faces* **321**.

529

You have found an explorer's book full of maps and handy hints. Add 1 to your SCOUTING score. Also roll one die, and if you get higher than your Rank you go up one Rank. (Going up in Rank means that your unwounded Stamina score increases by 1–6. Also your Defense will go up by 1.)

Hearing an ominous sound from the back of the library, you hurry out of the castle. Turn to **314**.

530

Sir Debrumas visits you in your cell. Pressing a perfumed scarf to his face to cover the overpowering stench, he says: "The Baroness will grant you freedom if you will pay a ransom of 300 Shards."

Agree to pay 300 Shards	turn to **229**
Refuse	turn to **555**

531

"The Watcher was a knight who made a pact with the demonic gods of the Uttakin," says Knocklar. "He thought he'd get eternal life, but instead he became a corpse that could not quite die. He lies in his crypt dreaming of treasure and lost hopes."

"Where is his crypt?"

"Here in this very forest. A stone tomb with a pyramid above it. The green jewel in the pyramid resembles an eye, and it's that jewel that gives the undead knight his name."

"How much is the jewel worth?" you wonder.

Knocklar scowls. "I'll tell you what it's not worth. It's not worth touching—not if you value your sanity! Now, I've got things I should be getting on with...."

Turn to **456**.

532

If your SANCTITY score is 6 or more, turn to **557**. If it is 5 or less, turn to **581**.

533

You are in the central part of the limestone mountains separating Golnir from the Great Steppes. If you have the codeword *Bunting*, turn to **518**. If not, turn to **543**.

534

You are forced to put out to sea to escape being dashed on the rocks. When the storm has passed, you take stock of the damage.

Quite a lot of things have been swept overboard. Your vessel has lost one Cargo Unit, if you were carrying cargo. (If you had several cargo units, you choose which was lost.)

"I don't know where we are, skipper," says the mate. "Way off course, that's for sure."

You look around. There is no sight of land. Turn to *Over the Blood-Dark Sea* **301**.

535

The pirates seize you and clap you in iron chains, then put your own vessel in tow and start the long haul back to their base.

Cross off your money, possessions, and any Cargo Units aboard your vessel. However, do not cross the ship off the Ship's Manifest just yet. You may still be able to escape from your captors...

Turn to *Over the Blood-Dark Sea* **454**.

536

You help yourself to the pirates' treasure, which amounts to 500 Shards. Record it on your Adventure Sheet. Their hold contains 1 Cargo Unit of furs, which you can add to your own cargo if you have room for it. Your mate advises taking the **pirate captain's head**: "A grisly trophy, perhaps, but often there's a reward if you have proof you've slain such a devil."

You also get a chance to increase in Rank after your stirring leadership in battle. Roll two dice, and if the result is greater than your current Rank you gain a Rank. You also gain 1–6 Stamina points *permanently*; increase your normal (unwounded) Stamina score by the roll of one die. Remember that going up a Rank increases your Defense.

Turn to **14**.

537

A mason who has been working at Castle Ravayne mentions that he is supposed to renovate the private citadel of Sir Bredubar, the Knight of the Long Knife. "I don't know why he thinks the place needs fortifying," says the mason. "Maybe he knows something I don't. Still, the money's good."

Get the codeword *Bobbin*. (If you already had it, get the codeword *Bisect* as well.) Then turn to **48**.

538

The pirate vessel crunches into the side of your ship and the attackers swarm aboard. Your men square off grimly with hooks, belaying pins, and anything else that comes to hand. They will die fighting rather than be enslaved.

Roll three dice if you are a Warrior, or two dice if you belong to any other profession. Add your Rank to this roll. Then, if your crew is poor quality, subtract 2 from the total. If the crew is good, add 2. If the crew is excellent, add 3.

Score 0–4	Calamity; you are killed	turn to **560**
Score 5–9	Crushing defeat; lose 2–12 Stamina	turn to **535**
Score 10–13	Forced to give in; lose 1–6 Stamina	turn to **510**
Score 14–17	The pirates withdraw	turn to **221**
Score 18+	Outright victory	turn to **563**

539

The smugglers are quite taken with your roguish ways. They share a glass of whiskey with you. Swapping stories, you learn that they brought some warriors from Akatsurai to these shores. "I had to show them the way through the Magwort Fens," volunteers one man. "I reckon they had a treasure they wanted to leave there."

Bidding the smugglers farewell, you set out again. Turn to **268**.

ESTRAGON THE WIZARD

540

"Why have you returned empty-handed?" cries Estragon irritably. "You are wasting my time. Begone!"

He claps his hands. There is a flash like a bolt of azure lightning and you are hurled through space, landing in a haystack. Roll one die to see where you've ended up:

Score 1–3	turn to **223**
Score 4–5	turn to **200**
Score 6	turn to **153**

541

"You bring glad tidings indeed!" says Vanna, clapping her hands in delight. "An alliance with the warriors of Akatsurai will help this realm prosper."

Roll two dice, and if the total is higher than your CHARISMA score increase it by 1. Vanna also orders her steward to reward you with 150 Shards out of the castle treasury.

Cross the **diplomatic letter** off your Adventure Sheet and turn to **342**.

542

"I have been waiting for you," Estragon says. "There is a task you can perform, and in return I'll teach you a little sorcery."

If the first box below is not marked, put a mark in it and then turn to **490**. Otherwise, continue down until you reach the first empty box, mark it and then turn to the number given.

❑	turn to **490**
❑	turn to **565**
❑	turn to **613**
If all boxes are marked	turn to **390**

543

No one has ever made a comprehensive map of these mountains. If you wish to attempt it, you will need to explore this region and the peaks extending off to the east. To do this, you must first possess a **parchment**. If you do, make a SCOUTING roll at a Difficulty of 15.

Successful SCOUTING roll	turn to **568**
Failed SCOUTING roll	turn to **592**
No parchment	turn to **518**

544

You try to convince the outlaws you are as ruthless and experienced as any of them. Unfortunately it comes out sounding like a hollow boast. Your miserable attempt at roguish nonchalance falls flat; your charm comes across like nervous prattling; the accounts of your crimes seem obviously to be lies.

One fellow with a scar running right across the bridge of his nose gives you a long hard stare and says: "What's got you jittery, pal? Couldn't be us, could it, mates? Sweet as lambs, we are!"

He rocks with laughter. But his eyes aren't laughing.

Suddenly they grab you, strip you of everything you possess, and pelt you with clumps of dirt until you are driven away. Cross all possessions and money off your Adventure Sheet, then turn to **172**.

545

A squat Trau waits with a broad grin as you go to leave the circle of stones. "That'll be one Mithral," it croaks, holding out a hairy paw.

Pay 1 Mithral	turn to **173**
Can't or won't pay	turn to **570**

546

You come across a goblin crouched on a toadstool. It is chewing a dead rat.

The blood dribbles down its chin as it looks at you, grins and says: "She works hard to fill her larder. Her mother dined after killing father."

"What's that?"

The goblin gobbles up the last bit of the rat. "Answer that riddle, and you'll know the safe door to take in the old fort on the coast."

Go east	turn to **496**
Go west	turn to **595**
Go south	turn to **124**
Go north	turn to **521**

547 ❑

If the box is empty, put a checkmark in it and turn to **572**. If the box is already marked, turn to **596**.

548

The Sokarans tell you that they work for a consortium of merchants in Yellowport.

"We are traveling around Golnir to find out what commodities are in demand," explains the senior member of the party. "Minerals are plentiful in Yellowport, as you may know, but grain and furs are in short supply."

Bidding them good-bye, you continue along the riverbank. Turn to **130**.

549

A group of travelers from Sokara rein in as they see you go by. If you have the title *King's Champion*, turn to **401**. If you have the title *Protector of Sokara*, turn to **426**. Otherwise turn to **287**.

550

You encounter a group of drunken louts on the road. They are passing around a jug of ale and singing:

"I'm off to Goldfall,
There to get rich,
And I'll marry a wife
And I'll call her *that wife!*
And when I've got money
And fine clothes that fit,
Folk will line up
Just to lick my *hand!*"

This song causes them such amusement that they do not even notice you go by. If they're typical of the people who go to Goldfall, it isn't worth staying there longer than you have to. Turn to **58**.

551

The nuns are disappointed that you have decided to leave their order. "May Lacuna watch over you and guide you back to the path of righteousness," says the Abbess. Turn to **38**.

552

It was almost too easy. Nestling down in a barn in the castle courtyard, you sleep peacefully through the rest of the night, dreaming of what you will do with your ill-gotten gains.

Roll two dice. If the total is higher than your THIEVERY score, increase it by 1. After doing that, turn to **315**.

553

The waves close over your head and your only thought now is to save yourself. Roll two dice. If the score is greater than your Rank, you are drowned. If the score is less than or equal to your Rank, you are swept miraculously toward the shore. Lose 1–6 Stamina points and, if you survive, turn to **559**.

554

It is a magician's book brimming with mysterious secrets. Roll two dice. Gain 1 on MAGIC if you get higher than your current score, but *lose* 1 MAGIC if you roll a two.

Hearing a floorboard creak at the back of the room, you hurriedly replace the book and leave. Turn to **314**.

555

Every few days, the jailer chains you to the wall and gives you a pounding. One day he goes too far and thinks he has killed you—and perhaps he has. Lose 1–6 Stamina points (the score of one die). If you survive, turn to **505**. If not, turn to **560**.

556

You learn that the Tower of Despair, which is commonly thought to stand on the edge of the Endless Plains, is in fact in this very forest. "It contains the treasure of an undead knight," says Knocklar. "He pledged half of what he had to gain eternal life, and the other half he locked in that tower."

"A considerable sum, presumably."

"Enough to make every king despair, and every merchant weep with greed! But forget about stealing it. The only way to open the tower is with the key of stars, which is in the hands of the Trau King of the Whistling Heath."

Knocklar has no more time for gossip. He has to be getting on with his chores. Turn to **456**.

557

A squirrel comes scampering up to you. It watches you with large luminous eyes, head cocked quizzically. Then, to your great surprise, it speaks: "My lords and ladies of the wildwood crave a favor. Your presence annoys them. Your aura is the cause of discomfort. The odor of violets is one they cannot abide."

All of this means nothing to you. But then, the fact that a squirrel can talk at all is miracle enough. You can hardly expect it to talk sense.

"If you would leave the glade now, my lords and ladies can take their repast," says the squirrel more plainly. "To compensate for the inconvenience to yourself, they offer a pot of fine fairy mead, which you will find inside the hollow tree trunk behind you."

You reach into the tree trunk. There is indeed a pot of **fairy mead**. You take it and, not wishing to incur the elves' displeasure, return along the path without delay. Turn to **22**.

558

Five swarthy brigands leap out from the hedge at the side of the road. They are masked with silk scarves, but you can hear the sneers as they raise their swords and demand: "Your money or your life!"

Fight them	turn to **582**
Run off	turn to **606**
Hand over your cash	turn to **630**

559

You wake to find you have been washed up on a beach. Cold rain pours down on the sea breeze. You are dazed and bleeding, but lucky to be alive. Turn to **705**.

560

You are dead. If you previously made arrangements for resurrection, turn to the appropriate section. If not, this is the end.

561

As you trudge across the pebbles by the water's edge, a breeze blows in from out at sea, bringing the faintly heard strains of flute music.

"What's that?" you ask the fishermen.

"It's from the belfry of the old village that now lies out under the sea," replies the older man. "At low tide you can see the roofs of the buildings. Walk out to them, even."

"Not that anyone would," puts in the other man with a shudder.

"Flute music—from a belfry?"

"They never had a bell, see. A fellow called folk to prayer with his flute. They say he was still playing when the sea closed over his head."

Continue along the beach	turn to **585**
Return to the top of the cliff	turn to **373**

562

A group of merchants are huddled at the dockside discussing the political situation in Yellowport. "I'm withdrawing my investments," says one. "There'll be anarchy in the streets before the year is out, you mark my words!" Turn to **48**.

563

You help yourself to the pirates' treasure, which amounts to 950 Shards. Record it on your Adventure Sheet. Their ship's hold contains 1 Cargo Unit of spices, which you can add to your own cargo if you have room. Your mate advises taking the **pirate captain's head**: "A grisly trophy, perhaps, but often there's a reward if you have proof you've slain such a devil."

You also get a chance to increase in Rank. Roll two dice, and if the result is greater than your current Rank you gain a Rank. You also gain 1–6 Stamina points *permanently;* increase your normal (unwounded) Stamina score by the roll of one die. Remember that going up a Rank increases your Defense.

Turn to **221**.

564

They fear you might tell the authorities about them. Three of them step forward slowly, moving with the slow crablike crouch of wrestlers. You get ready to fight, but you did not notice the smuggler creeping up behind you. He dashes a large stone against your skull and you fall stunned.

The smugglers demand a ransom of 100 Shards to let you go. Otherwise they intend to tie you up and put you aboard the Uttakin ship that brought their contraband.

Pay the ransom	turn to **229**
Can't or won't pay	*The Court of Hidden Faces* **321**

565

"I can do nothing until I acquire a mermaid's **coral-red tresses**," Estragon tells you. "I'll teach you some more of my magic when you bring me what I need."

"Where will I find a mermaid?"

He gives you a sharp look. "Not in the northern hills, that's for sure."

Turn to **342**.

566

"The mountains of the north are said to be the broken backbone of the dead god Harkun, who lies across the width of the world," says Vanna. "Most people do not dare to venture there, and no map has ever been made showing the paths, valleys and hidden passes."

You nod to show you understand. "I shall bring you that map, my lady."

Turn to **342**.

567

You tell Estragon you have brought him an item he needs for his experiments. Before turning to the entry listed here, put a checkmark in the box to remind yourself that you've completed that errand. (You can't run the same errand twice!)

scarab amulet ❑	turn to **515**
coral-red tresses ❑	turn to **589**
golden katana ❑	turn to **637**
None of these items	turn to **540**
If all boxes marked	turn to **390**

568

After several days you have the beginnings of a chart showing the passes and trails through the mountains. Get the codeword *Buzz* and turn to **518**.

569

While you sleep, the ghost gnaws at your leg. Having died of starvation, it is driven to eternally crave flesh. You feel nothing, but the ghost is not sated until you have lost 3–18 Stamina points (roll three dice). If you can survive that, you wake at dawn to find your leg horribly mauled. Only then do you recall the wispy gray visitation that at the time you took to be a dream. Turn to **172**.

570

The Trau bundle you into a hamper and drag you down under the earth with them, and that is the last that is ever seen of you.

571

You are lucky enough to find a **four-leaf clover**. Surely this is a good omen.

Go east	turn to **496**
Go west	turn to **396**
Go south	turn to **124**
Go north	turn to **195**

572

Behind the door is a copper chest containing 300 Shards, **ring mail (Defense +2)** and a **compass (SCOUTING +1)**. After making a note of anything you want to take, decide whether to try one of the other doors or leave.

Open the left-hand door	turn to **497**
Open the central door	turn to **522**
Leave the fort	turn to **373**

573

Just after nightfall, a raft carrying translucent figures comes drifting along the river. "Come with us," call out the wraiths.

"We'll take you to a feast in the underworld."

Climb aboard	turn to **603**
Shun them	turn to **130**

574

The knight is searching for the lady to whom he has pledged his courtly love. "She was abducted by a villainous knight," he growls. "I'll soon wreak revenge when I learn where he's taken her."

If you have the codeword *Bridoon*, turn to **451**. If you have the codeword *Brisket*, turn to **476**. If you have neither codeword, turn to **31**.

575

"Who asked for your opinion?" growls the tusked head. The other two heads, however, think you have a point. A fierce argument ensues, and finally the red-eyed head butts the tusked head so hard that both are knocked out.

You climb out of the net and start to walk away. The troll holds up a finger uncertainly. "Er...excuse me," says the tiny head, "but what am I going to say to Tusker and Stareface when they wake up?"

"Tell them to stick to eating rabbits in the future."

Turn to **246**.

576

You can rest at the abbey as long as is necessary to recover from your injuries. Restore your Stamina to its normal unwounded score. When you are ready to resume your travels, turn to **38**.

577

"Stop, thief!"

You have no intention of doing anything of the sort. You know only too well the fate that awaits you if you're caught. Abandoning part of your haul to delay the sentries (lose 400 Shards), you race out of the castle gates into the night.

Get the codeword *Bullion* and turn to **118**.

578

A thin gray figure clad in decaying robes comes stalking forward out of the cold dank heart of the mound. It wears a belt of shrunken human heads, and from the way it is brandishing that knife you suspect it wants to add your own head to its collection.

Run	turn to **602**
Fight	turn to **626**
Call on your god (if you have one)	turn to **650**

579

It is a cursed book, written by a madman with the sole purpose of bringing chaos to the world. Unless you are an initiate of Lacuna, you forget who you are and are reduced to 1st Rank. Lose all codewords in this book except *Baluster*, *Bosky*, *Bullion*, and *Bashful* if you have them. Roll two dice; the total is your new unwounded Stamina score. (Be glad that your other abilities are not affected as well.)

Struck by sudden terror, you flee from the castle. Turn to **314**.

580

A huge golden-skinned snake dangles from the branch in front of you. A green gem is set into the middle of its head. As this burns against the twilight, you hear a voice in your mind, all cold hisses and dripping with predatory nuance: *Hear me, mortal. You seek adventure? Hazards hold no terror for you? Then submit to my wager....*

Accept the snake's wager	turn to **652**
Attack it	turn to **604**
Run off	turn to **93**

581

An elfin lady encased in elegant silver armor leaps forward from the undergrowth. Smiling sweetly, but without speaking a word, she levels her longsword and lunges at you.

Elf Lady, COMBAT 7, Defense 10, Stamina 7

You doubt if she'd accept your surrender. If you turn and run, she will get one final swipe at your undefended back and you will lose 1–6 Stamina points.

Fight and defeat her	turn to **605**
Run off	turn to **22**

582

This will not be an easy fight, but at least the brigands have the decency to line up and fight you one at a time. Indeed, they seem almost amused by the "sport."

First Brigand, COMBAT 4, Defense 6, Stamina 4

Second Brigand, COMBAT 4, Defense 6, Stamina 3

Third Brigand, COMBAT 4, Defense 6, Stamina 4

Fourth Brigand, COMBAT 4, Defense 6, Stamina 3

Fifth Brigand, COMBAT 4, Defense 7, Stamina 5

It's too late to think of running away, but you could try begging for mercy if things go against you.

Defeat them all	turn to **654**
Surrender	turn to **678**

583

Thick black clouds pile up along the horizon.

If you have the blessing of Alvir and Valmir, which confers Safety from Storms, you can ignore the storm. Cross off your blessing and turn to **198**.

Otherwise the storm hits with full fury. Roll one die if your ship is a barque, two dice if it is a brigantine, or three dice if a galleon. Add 1 to the roll if you have a good crew; add 2 if you have an excellent crew.

Score 1–3	Ship sinks	turn to **459**
Score 4–5	The mast splits	turn to **534**
Score 6–20	You weather the storm	turn to **14**

584

You help yourself to the pirates' treasure, which amounts to 800 Shards. Record it on your Adventure Sheet. Their ship's hold contains 1 Cargo Unit of spices, which you can add to your own cargo if you have room for it. Your mate advises taking the **pirate captain's head**: "A grisly trophy, perhaps, but often there's a reward if you have proof you've slain such a devil."

You also get a chance to increase in Rank after your stirring leadership in battle. Roll two dice, and if the result is greater than your current Rank you gain a Rank. You also gain 1–6 Stamina points *permanently*; increase your normal (unwounded) Stamina score by the roll of one die. Remember that going up a Rank increases your Defense.

Once you have made the necessary adjustments to your Adventure Sheet, turn to **335**.

585

You watch clouds scud across the sky. The breeze raises white-caps on the water and drives foamy waves up into the tide-pools. But for a few crabs and a circling gull or two, you are alone on this desolate stretch of shore.

Wait for low tide	turn to **609**
Go back up to the clifftops	turn to **373**

586 ❏

If the box above is empty, put a checkmark in it and turn to **658**. If it was marked already, turn to **634**.

587

The approaching vessel at first seemed to be an innocent merchantman, but then your lookout points to the banks of oars. "A pirate galley!" he cries. Sure enough, at that moment the ship hoists the red pennant of the Kingdom of the Reavers. Her oars give her a good burst of speed over short distances, and she is soon bearing down on you.

Make a run for it	turn to **611**
Parley	turn to **635**
Fight it out	turn to **659**

588

The knight reins in, waving his men to a halt. Raising his visor, he takes a close look at you, then shuffles through some wanted posters that the sergeant of militia hands to him. Then he gives a judicious nod, and before you can act the militia have seized you.

"Did you think you'd got away with your crime?" grates the knight. "The Baroness's justice has a long reach!"

You are divested of all your possessions and cash (cross them off) and hauled off in chains to Castle Ravayne, where they fling you into the dungeons. Turn to **365**.

589

"You have done well," says Estragon as he inspects the **coral-red tresses**.

In return for your service, he teaches you some spells from his grimoire. Roll two dice, and if the total is higher than your MAGIC score then you gain 1 point of MAGIC.

Remember to cross the **coral-red tresses** off your Adventure Sheet, then turn to **342**.

590

"Many of the towns of the north pay tribute to this noble house in return for protection," Vanna tells you. "But now a dragon has arisen which flies forth by night, disgorging fire upon the peasants' barns and carrying off their cattle."

Not without qualms, you reply: "Leave this to me, my lady."

I shall bring you the dragon's head, or you can take my own instead."

There is applause from the assembled knights and courtiers as you withdraw. Turn to **342**.

591

Roll one die to see what reward you are given:

Score 1-3	Training	turn to **615**
Score 4-5	Armor	turn to **639**
Score 6	A ship	turn to **663**

592

While trying to chart the extent of a river gorge, you slip and fall, taking an injury of 2–12 Stamina points (roll two dice). If you survive, turn to **518**.

593

Molhern's anvil is a large flat boulder planted firmly in the ground, sheltered by a few chestnut trees. Legend has it that you can leave weapons or armor here for the god to work on overnight.

If you want to leave something on the boulder, turn to **617**. If not, turn to **97**.

594

Following the merchant's advice, you invest your money and wait to see what return you get. Roll two dice:

Score 2-3	A con trick! Lose all your investment.
Score 4-5	Pirates attacked the ship. Lose half your investment.
Score 6-7	Another shipment arrives. No gain or loss.
Score 8-9	A roaring spice trade doubles your investment.
Score 10-12	Your money is increased threefold!

After making any changes on your Adventure Sheet, turn to **48**.

595

You are attacked without warning by an ogre who runs out from his hiding place behind one of the tors.

Ogre, COMBAT 5, Defense 8, Stamina 10

If you run away, the ogre will get a final swipe at your retreating back, inflicting 1–6 Stamina points of injury.

| Run away | turn to **124** |
| Kill the ogre | turn to **496** |

596

You are bitten by a large spider which drops from the door handle onto your wrist. Its venom causes your hand to go stiff, the fingers permanently crooked. Lose 1 from your COMBAT score unless you have a blessing of Immunity to Disease and Poison.

There is nothing else here.

Open the left-hand door	turn to **497**
Open the central door	turn to **522**
Leave the fort	turn to **373**

597

A rangy, unshaven fellow with a broad grin catches up as you are walking along a lane and proposes a contest of holiness. "I'll wager everything I've got against everything you've got," he says cheerily.

"What *have* you got?"

He shows you a diamond worth at least 600 Shards. "Is it a deal?"

| Accept the wager | turn to **783** |
| Refuse and bid him good-bye | turn to **153** |

598

You pass a man whose cart has lost a wheel. "If I can't get it fixed then I'll miss the market!" he wails, but no one will stop to help.

| Help him fix the wheel | turn to **438** |
| Pass by | turn to **31** |

599

A lady calls to you from the window of a fortified tower as you pass by below.

"I've been abducted by an evil knight," she says. "If you see my champion, pray tell him where I am."

"Do you need rescuing?" you call back.

"Thank you for the offer, but I think my champion will want to do that himself."

| Rescue her | turn to **413** |
| Go on your way | turn to **388** |

600

A mist creeps in on the sea breeze, swirling in pockets across the downs. Hearing a footfall, you look back nervously, but the mist makes it impossible to see if you are being followed.

Make a SCOUTING roll at a Difficulty of 13.

| Successful SCOUTING roll | turn to **425** |
| Failed SCOUTING roll | turn to **675** |

601

You settle down in the common room for a drink. There is a familiar face at the next table. It is one of the brigands who robbed you! With a cry of rage, you give him a hearty blow with the bottom of your tankard.

Brigand, COMBAT 4, Defense 5, Stamina 2

You ought to be able to beat him after getting the first blow. Assuming you win, you can take the 25 Shards he has on him. Then you had better leave before the militiamen turn up and start asking questions. Turn to **189**.

602

The creature chases you through the night. To stay ahead of it, you must make a SCOUTING roll at a Difficulty of 14.

| Successful SCOUTING roll | turn to **722** |
| Failed SCOUTING roll | turn to **626** |

603

As the raft drifts on, darkness congeals around you until the only things you can see are the ghostly figures beside you. Finally the raft jolts to a halt, and you walk along a jetty into a shadowy hall. Turn to **689**.

604

You are locked in battle with a golden serpent that hangs from the branches overhead. Its coils are wound around you, leaving you with no chance to flee.

Jeweled Serpent, COMBAT 7, Defense 8, Stamina 9

If you kill it, turn to **628**.

605

She falls onto your sword. You recoil in horror as she pulls herself along it, gladly embracing death, digging her fingers into your shoulders and planting an icy kiss on your brow.

Your senses slowly fall away. For a time there is fleeting oblivion, like the state at the edge of sleep. You are dimly aware of voices, fugitive sights and sounds, but they quickly fade.

Then you find yourself looking into the kindly face of a nun. She wears the silver-trimmed white habit of a devotee of the goddess Lacuna. "Where am I?" you ask.

She smiles. "In our abbey. You were found raving in the countryside, and some pilgrims brought you to us. Thank the goddess that your sanity has at last returned."

You soon find that a year and a day has passed without you having any recollection. You have lost all the possessions that you were carrying when you encountered the elfin lady, and all your money has gone too. However, from somewhere you have acquired a **silver horseshoe**, an **inkpot,** and a **fishing hook**. Note these as your sole possessions, then turn to **61**.

606

You leap over the hedge, but get tangled up long enough for the two nearest brigands to slash at you with their swords. Lose 2–12 Stamina points (the score of two dice) and, if you survive, you beat a hasty retreat. Turn to **78**.

607

Thick black clouds pile up along the horizon.

If you have the blessing of Alvir and Valmir, which confers Safety from Storms, you can ignore the storm. Cross off your blessing and turn to **221**.

Otherwise the storm hits with full fury. Roll one die if your ship is a barque, two dice if it is a brigantine, or three dice if a galleon. Add 1 to the roll if you have a good crew; add 2 if you have an excellent crew.

Score 1–3	Ship sinks	turn to **459**
Score 4–5	The mast splits	turn to **534**
Score 6–20	You weather the storm	turn to **358**

608

The approaching vessel at first seemed to be an innocent merchantman, but then your lookout points to the banks of oars. "A pirate galley!" he cries. Sure enough, at that moment the ship hoists the red pennant of the Kingdom of the Reavers. Her oars give her a good burst of speed over short distances, and she is soon bearing down on you.

Make a run for it	turn to **632**
Parley	turn to **656**
Fight it out	turn to **680**

609

If you have the codeword *Boysen*, turn to **633**. If not, turn to **657**.

610

Tekshin charges 2 Shards a day for board and lodging. Each day you spend here, you can recover 1 Stamina point if injured, up to the limit of your normal unwounded Stamina score. When you are ready to leave, turn to **356**.

611

Roll two dice and add your Rank. Subtract 1 from the total if you have a poor crew, add 1 if you have a good crew, add 2 if you have an excellent crew.

Score 1-6	The pirates overtake you	turn to **659**
Score 7+	You outrun them	turn to **198**

612

You see the mermaids leaping between the crests of the waves. The bubbling music of their laughter is a poignant and captivating sound. "Better leave them be, captain," warns the mate. "If they take offense they can lay a curse on the ship."

Speak to the mermaids	turn to **636**
Sail on	turn to **335**

613

"Now I need a **golden katana**," says Estragon.

"A what?"

"It is the sword of one of the knights who serve the Chancellor of the land of Akatsurai, which lies far across the ocean to the southeast. Go, and when you return I will impart the inner arcana of the mystic arts."

Surely there must be somewhere nearer than Akatsurai where you can get hold of the item you need? Turn to **342**.

614

There is a gasp from everyone present when you unroll your cape and show what you have brought.

"It is a marvel!" cries Vanna, leaping to her feet. "Truly you are as great as any knight of this court."

Roll two dice, and if the result is greater than your current Rank you gain a Rank. You also gain 1–6 Stamina points *permanently;* increase your normal (unwounded) Stamina score by the roll of one die. Remember that going up a Rank increases your Defense.

Also, Vanna takes her sword and knights you on the spot. You are given the title *Paladin of Ravayne* and assured that you will always be welcome here.

Remember to cross the **dragon's head** off your Adventure Sheet, then turn to **342**.

615

Vanna commands the most skilled instructors in her service to teach you whatever you wish. Select one of your abilities (COMBAT, MAGIC, etc.) and roll one die. If the number rolled is higher than your score in the ability, add 1 to it.

Turn to **342**.

616

Lose the codeword *Buzz*. You are determined to finish your map. Make a SCOUTING roll at a Difficulty of 15.

Successful SCOUTING roll	turn to **736**
Failed SCOUTING roll	turn to **712**

617

Decide which item you are leaving here. (It must be either a weapon or a suit of armor.) You also have to leave a sum of money to pay the god for his services; decide how much.

You camp out for the night not far away. Sometime after midnight you are awakened by a hammering sound from the other side of the trees.

Investigate	turn to **641**
Go back to sleep	turn to **665**

618

You hide behind a stack of crates on the dock and wait for night to give you the cover you'll need. Make a THIEVERY roll at a Difficulty of 12.

Successful THIEVERY roll	turn to **730**
Failed THIEVERY roll	turn to **439**

619

The next morning, your 50 Shards has gone but in its place you find a jar of **fairy mead**. Add this to your list of possessions and turn to **349**.

620

You make your way to a camp where a bevy of beautiful young dancers are cavorting around in the firelight. Their footsteps are so light that they hardly make the dry leaves rustle at all.

If you have the codeword *Bones*, turn to **209**. Otherwise turn to **37**.

621

At dusk, seeing a light ahead, you quicken your pace and arrive at an inn. An old peeling sign hangs outside it, creaking in the wind. As you approach, the door opens and the innkeeper beckons you to enter. "It's a cold and blustery night to be out," he says.

Enter the inn	turn to **679**
Pass by	turn to **153**

622

The priests give you some advice on religious rituals that might stand you in good stead. Roll one die, and if you get higher than your SANCTITY score you can add 1 to it. Bidding the priests farewell, you continue on your way. Turn to **127**.

623

You witness a group of soldiers executing a criminal by means of an old ordeal called the Blood Eagle. This involves cutting open the chest and draping the lungs back over the shoulders like gory wings. It takes the victim quite some time to die. You find the spectacle so salutary that you lose 1 from your THIEVERY score. Turn to **223**.

624

You steal into the keep after nightfall. To break into the treasury chamber, you must make a THIEVERY roll at a Difficulty of 15.

Successful THIEVERY roll	turn to **502**
Failed THIEVERY roll	turn to **527**

625

Chard charges 2 Shards a day for board and lodging. Each day you spend here, you can recover 1 Stamina point if injured, up to the limit of your normal unwounded Stamina score.

When you are ready to leave, turn to **189**.

626

The creature gives a laugh of unholy glee and rushes at you.

Barrow Wight, COMBAT 5, Defense 9, Stamina 18

There is no point in fleeing. You could never escape from it now that night has fallen. If you win, turn to **698**.

627

Guffawing, the sprites let you go. You run pell-mell until there's no breath left in you. Only then do you notice that they stole one of your fingers. Lose 1 from THIEVERY (down to a minimum score of 1) and turn to **288**.

628

A **green gem** is set into the serpent's head. It takes all your strength to pry it out of the bone in which it is set, but at last you manage it. You can sell the **green gem** for 100 Shards at any market (note that on your Adventure Sheet so you remember) or you can keep it. Turn to **116**.

629

"That would be fractious little Nivram," says Knocklar after hearing your account. "He's got it into his head to learn great sorcery, but he's really just a bumbler who relies on other wizards' inventions."

You nod. "So he's no great threat, then?"

Knocklar raises his eyebrows. "Oh, I wouldn't say that. Once you've got on the wrong side of him he'll use any amount of treacherous scheming to try to get his own back."

There is no more opportunity for gossip. It is time you were on your way. Turn to **456**.

630

Cross off all the money you are carrying. The leader of the brigands gives a gallant bow and says, "Our thanks, stranger. It is rare to encounter such generosity in these perilous times."

With a mocking laugh, the scoundrels run off. Get the codeword *Bounty* and turn to **258**.

631

Cross the **fishing hook** off your Adventure Sheet.

The fishermen are so relieved at not having to face their wives empty-handed that they spend the rest of the morning teaching you how to fish. Try to roll higher than your current SCOUTING score on two dice, and if you succeed you can increase your SCOUTING by 1.

You bid the fishermen farewell. Turn to **371**.

632

Roll two dice and add your Rank. Subtract 1 from the total if you have a poor crew. Add 1 if you have a good crew. Add 2 if you have an excellent crew.

Score 1-6	The pirates overtake you	turn to **680**
Score 7+	You outrun them	turn to **358**

633

If you have the codewords *Bastion* or *Brush*, delete them and the codeword *Boysen* and then turn to **657**. Otherwise turn to **681**.

634

You strike up a conversation with a dwarf who is going in the same direction. He works as a jester in the wintertime, usually spending a month at each castle he visits. "My jokes and tricks mean I am much in demand."

"And in the summer?"

"Alas, no one has time for feasts when the weather is fine."

His friendly wit inspires you. Roll one die, and if you get higher than your CHARISMA score then add 1 to it. Then turn to **223**.

635

The pirates pull alongside and cast grappling hooks to seize your vessel. Within moments they are swarming aboard. You offer them your goods, but plead for the freedom of your crew. Make a CHARISMA roll at a Difficulty of 15.

Successful CHARISMA roll	turn to **510**
Failed CHARISMA roll	turn to **535**

636

A particularly striking mermaid with a winsome face, coral curls, and a firm, lithe tail swims daringly close to the side of the ship. The mate grins at her and gives a friendly wave, but under his breath he says to you: "I reckon we could net the little imp, captain."

Talk to her	turn to **660**
Try to catch her in a net	turn to **684**
Continue on your way	turn to **335**

637

Estragon smiles. "I never thought you'd succeed in this quest."

"I thought you could see the future in your magic mirrors," you reply, handing him the **golden katana**.

"In this case the visions were unclear."

Roll two dice, and if the result is greater than your current Rank you gain a Rank. You also gain 1–6 Stamina points *permanently;* increase your normal (unwounded) Stamina score by the roll of one die. Remember that going up a Rank increases your Defense.

Remember to cross the **golden katana** off your Adventure Sheet, then turn to **342**.

638

"This chart will be useful to our soldiers if there should be any danger from the nomad hordes of the deep north," says Vanna.

"You have served me well."

Roll two dice, and if the total is higher than your SCOUTING score increase it by 1. Vanna also orders her steward to reward you with 50 Shards out of the castle treasury.

Cross the **map of the mountains** off your Adventure Sheet and turn to **342**.

639

You are presented with a suit of **splint armor (Defense +4)**. This is decorated with the crest of the Ravayne family, and it would be an insult to Vanna if you declined to wear it at all times. Lose any other suits of armor that you have in your possession (Sir Debrumas takes them to give to the Poor Knights' Fund).

Turn to **342**.

640

If you have the codeword *Buzz*, turn to **616**. If not, turn to **712**.

641

The hammering gets louder as you approach. Sparks fly on the night wind. You see the shadow of a huge man against the foliage.

You step on a twig. The crack is followed by dead silence.

You continue on to the clearing. The money and item you left have gone. Cross them off your Adventure Sheet.

And yet …

You feel the boulder. It's still warm.

Turn to **97**.

642

You are wandering across the gloomy dales of the Whistling Heath.

Go north	turn to **496**
Go south	turn to **421**
Go east	turn to **521**
Go west	turn to **546**

643

You wait all night, going back to the hole to see what has been left for you. The pot and your 50 Shards have gone, but there is a **silver mirror**.

When you look into the mirror, however, you are horrified to see that your face has been frightfully rearranged. You now look like something out of a nightmare. Reduce your CHARISMA to 1 and note that it can *never* increase again.

Sick at heart, you trudge on through the woods. Turn to **349**.

644

You make the acquaintance of a friendly fellow who accompanies you on your journey and entertains you with his jokes. Make a THIEVERY roll at a Difficulty of 13.

Successful THIEVERY roll	turn to **40**
Failed THIEVERY roll	turn to **774**

645

You come across an old bogle laughing to himself. His body looks like a mossy old tree stump and he has a mouth as wide as a sack of coal. When you ask why he's laughing, he replies: "Because there you are gaping instead of running away, and now I'm about to up and eat you." If you have the codeword *Bookworm*, turn to **479**. If not, turn to **501**.

646

Three knights overtake you on the road. Over their armor they wear white shrouds, and their shields bear the holy device of the god of death. "We are pledged to Nagil," they say. "We count ourselves already dead, and so we cannot be defeated in battle for we have no fear."

They offer to make you an initiate of Nagil on the spot.

Accept the offer	turn to **512**
Refuse	turn to **127**

647

"Let's have none of that!" say the three heads when they see you clambering out of the net. The troll is on you instantly brandishing his cleaver.

Troll, COMBAT 8, Defense 12, Stamina 12

If you win you can take the **meat cleaver** and **net** and continue on your way. Turn to **246**.

648 ❑

If the box is empty, put a checkmark in it and turn to **672**. If it is already marked, turn to **716**.

649

Perhaps you didn't realize that professional bullfighters have an unfair advantage. The animals they fight have already been tired out and weakened by loss of blood. You are not likely to defeat a healthy bull, no matter how tough you are!

Enraged Bull, COMBAT 10, Defense 11, Stamina 40

If you win, turn to **673**. If you run for it, turn to **697**

650

You raise your arms, make the sacred gesture of your faith, and declare in a firm voice: "Away thee, crypt-spawned fiend!"

Make a SANCTITY roll at a Difficulty of 16.

Successful SANCTITY roll	turn to **674**
Failed SANCTITY roll	turn to **626**

651

"What a kind person you are," she says, clutching your sleeve. "So I'll reward you with a hint. If you go to Castle Orlock, be sure to join the temple of Lacuna first."

Pulling away, you resume your journey. Turn to **35**.

652

The gem in the snake's head flares briefly, dazzling you. As your vision clears you see six wooden doorways set into the bank of earth beside you. Somehow you failed to notice them before.

One of these doors leads to vast treasure, the snake's telepathic voice informs you. *The others all conceal a ghastly doom. Choose one....*

The doors look the same. There is nothing to say which has the treasure behind it. Make a MAGIC roll at a Difficulty of 14.

Successful MAGIC roll	turn to **676**
Failed MAGIC roll	turn to **700**

653

You encounter seven fools who are engaged in a preposterous venture. Roll a die:

Score 1	turn to **677**
Score 2	turn to **701**
Score 3	turn to **725**
Score 4	turn to **749**
Score 5	turn to **773**
Score 6	turn to **383**

654

You ought to have learned a few new tricks in that fight. Roll two dice. If the total is higher than your Rank, you gain a Rank. Going up in Rank gives you an additional 1–6 Stamina points (added to both your current and unwounded Stamina scores) and will also increase your Defense by 1.

Searching the bodies of the brigands, you find four suits of **leather armor (Defense +1)**, one suit of **ring mail (Defense +2)**, five **swords,** and a purse containing 37 Shards.

Turn to **258**.

655

You give them directions to the abbey. The goddess must be pleased at this, because you receive the benefit of her blessing. In the Blessings box on your Adventure Sheet, write *SCOUTING re-roll (once only)*. The blessing works by allowing you to make a second attempt at a SCOUTING roll that you've failed. Whether or not the re-roll works, the blessing is then used up. Now turn to **355**.

656

The pirates pull alongside and cast grappling hooks to seize your vessel. Within moments they are swarming aboard. You offer them your goods, but plead for the freedom of your crew. Make a CHARISMA roll at a Difficulty of 15.

Successful CHARISMA roll	turn to **510**
Failed CHARISMA roll	turn to **535**

657

A huge shaggy warhorse with a coat of kelp and eyes like phosphor comes galloping out of the deep to attack you. There is no point in running—it would soon outdistance you. You must fight.

Ekushka, COMBAT 6, Defense 7, Stamina 10

If you win, turn to **705**.

658

You are drinking at a tavern when you notice a familiar face peering at you from behind a curtain. However, when you go over and throw back the curtain, there is no one to be seen.

Later you notice a chalky taste in your beer. Too late, you realize it is poisoned! If you have a blessing of Immunity to Disease and Poison then you are all right (remember to cross off the blessing now that it's used up). Without that blessing, the poison causes your skin to break out in gray blotches; lose 1–6 from your CHARISMA (down to a minimum score of 1).

After altering your Adventure Sheet if you need to, turn to **223**.

659

The pirate vessel crunches into the side of your ship. The attackers swarm aboard, screaming the war cry that has struck terror into many brave hearts over the centuries. Your men square off grimly with hooks, belaying pins, and anything else that comes to hand. They will die fighting rather than be enslaved.

Roll three dice if you are a Warrior, or two dice if you belong to any other profession. Add your Rank to this roll.

Then, if your crew is poor quality, subtract 2 from the total. If the crew is good quality, add 2. If the crew is excellent quality, add 3.

Score 0-4	Calamity; you are killed	turn to **560**
Score 5-9	Crushing defeat; lose 2-12 Stamina	turn to **535**
Score 10-13	Forced to give in; lose 1-6 Stamina	turn to **510**
Score 14-17	The pirates withdraw	turn to **198**
Score 18+	Outright victory	turn to **683**

660

The mermaid trills with merriment, but does not seem to understand your words. You must impress her with your innate charm, otherwise she will get bored and swim off. Make a CHARISMA roll at a Difficulty of 14.

Successful CHARISMA roll	turn to **708**
Failed CHARISMA roll	turn to **335**

661

Your chamber contains a plush four-poster bed where you can rest after your travels. The best food and drink is brought to you. If you are wounded, restore your Stamina to its normal unwounded score.

In one corner of the room is a locker where you can leave money or possessions for safekeeping. To do this, just cross the item off your Adventure Sheet and write it in the locker box here. Similarly, you can take any money or possessions you left here earlier.

Locker Box

When you are ready to leave your chamber, turn to **342**.

662

You present the Baroness with 100 Shards (or all that you're carrying, if you don't have that much on you). "What is mere wealth?" you declare gallantly. "I exist only to serve you, my lady."

Sir Debrumas accepts the money on Vanna's behalf, as it is not seemly for one of high noble birth to handle coins, You are escorted from the court and fetched back later for a banquet. If injured, recover 1 Stamina point (up to the limit of your normal unwounded score).

The next day you awaken refreshed and ready for any adventure. Turn to **342**.

663

Vanna tells you that a ship has been made ready for you in Ringhorn harbor. "Now perhaps you can do something about those dreadful Reavers," she says. "I'm told they prey on any ship that comes close to their shores."

Note on the Ship's Manifest that you now have a barque docked at Ringhorn. The crew is of average quality.

Turn to **342**.

664

A thick serpentine body with many heads rises up from behind the rocks. The venom spilling from its jaws produces plumes of acidic vapor where it touches the ground.

Fight the hydra	turn to **267**
Run away	turn to **290**

665

The next day you go back to see what has become of the item you left. The money has gone, as you expected. Roll two dice (three dice if you're an initiate of Molhern) and add 1 for every full 300 Shards you left as payment:

Score 2-6	The item has gone
Score 7-9	The item is unchanged
Score 10-12	The item is upgraded by +1
Score 13-15	The item is upgraded by +2
Score 16-18	The item is upgraded by +3
Score 19-21	The item is upgraded by +4
Score 22+	The item is upgraded by +5

An upgrade on armor increases its Defense bonus; an upgrade on a weapon increases its COMBAT bonus.

When you have made the necessary adjustments to your Adventure Sheet, turn to **97**.

666

The sigh of the wind as it swirls around the peaks sounds like the sharp intake of breath between the teeth of a giant.

Go north	turn to **571**
Go south	turn to **521**
Go east	turn to **546**
Go west	turn to **396**

667

His story concerns a man who found a copper pot under a tree stump. He wisely left a little silver in this, and was rewarded with health and good luck. He told his lazy brother about the pot, and he did the same. But the brother wasn't content with just health and luck, so he tried to bribe the fairy folk with bigger and bigger gifts. Finally they gave him a wart so big that it covered his whole face.

A cautionary tale that certainly seems to have quieted the local children down. Get the codeword *Blemish* and turn to **235**.

668

If you have the codeword *Blemish*, turn to **682**. If not, turn to **706**.

669

You meet a thatcher who is giggling to himself about how much money he's making. He explains his technique over a flagon of cider: "I arrive in a village and sell shares in the thatching of the roofs."

You're puzzled. "But surely you don't own the roofs? The villagers do."

"Ah, but then I point out that if they buy shares in a *neighbor's* roof, they'll be able to charge him rent."

"People would have to be stupid to fall for that!"

He grins. "Good thing they are, then. I make a pretty penny selling people their own roofs, I can tell you."

Perhaps you're in the wrong line of work. Turn to **265**.

670

A pirate ship bears down on you without warning. To your amazement, the captain decides to stand and fight. "I'll not run from these sea dogs!" he snarls. Roll three dice and add 3:

Score 6-13	You're defeated; lose	
	1-6 Stamina	turn to **510**
Score 14+	The pirates withdraw	*The War-Torn Kingdom* **140**

671

If you have the codeword *Baluster*, turn to **586**. If not, turn to **634**.

672

Plucking at your sleeves with damp ethereal fingers, the spirits lead you to shallow water below the torrent. Here you can see a heavy jade ring set into the riverbed. When you pull it, the waterfall miraculously stops as though a tap had been turned off. In the rock face beyond, there are two caves.

Enter the right-hand cave	turn to **696**
Enter the left-hand cave	turn to **720**
Leave now	turn to **716**

673

"Hey you!" cries an incredulous voice. "What are you doing?"

You look up from the carcass of the dead bull. "This bull attacked me…"

"Course it did!" says the farmer. "Didn't you have enough sense to stay out of its field? That was my prize bull, I'll have you know. I've a good mind to send for the militia."

He forces you to pay 150 Shards as compensation. (If you don't have that much, give him whatever you have.) Still, at least you get the chance to increase your COMBAT score by 1 if you can roll higher than your current COMBAT on two dice.

Then turn to **199**.

674

The barrow wight is held at bay, allowing you to make your escape. Turn to **222**.

675

A heavy hand descends on your shoulder. Hot blood-soaked breath warms your neck but chills your spine. If you have a **peacock feather**, turn to **699**. Otherwise you are gobbled up suddenly by the fiend and that is the end of you, turn to **560**.

676

The snake does not notice you cast a swift dowsing spell. Now you know which door leads to the treasure. You point to it confidently.

Again the gem flickers with light. Slowly four of the other doors creak open, each revealing a poison-tipped dart that would have slain you if you had chosen that door. *Now only two doors remain unopened*, says the snake telepathically. *Do you wish to stick to your original choice? I'll give you a last chance to change your mind.*

Stick with your first choice	turn to **748**
Choose the other closed door instead	turn to **724**

677

The simpletons are trying to get their cow to climb up a ladder on to the roof of their house, where they have noticed some stalks of grass growing in the thatch.

"Go on, Daisy!" urges one of the seven fools, giving the reluctant cow a shove.

"Why don't you climb the ladder, cut the grass, and throw it down to the cow?" you suggest.

They are so pleased that they invite you to stay with them for a few days. If injured, you can recover 1–6 Stamina points (roll one die for how many) before setting out on your way. Turn to **265**

678

The brigands accept your surrender. They take all your cash and, for good measure, also divest you of your possessions. You are left with scarcely a scrap of cloth to cover yourself.

"Next time you'll know not to be so argumentative," says the leader of the brigands as they run off.

Cross all cash and possessions off your Adventure Sheet, then turn to **258**.

679 ❑

If the box is empty, put a checkmark in it and turn to **703**. If the box was marked already, turn to **727**.

680

The prow of the pirate vessel crunches into your ship's side. The attackers swarm aboard, screaming the war cry that has struck terror into many brave hearts over the centuries. Your men square off grimly with hooks, belaying pins, and anything else that comes to hand. They will die fighting rather than be enslaved.

Roll three dice if you are a Warrior, or two dice if you belong to any other profession. Add your Rank to this roll.

Then, if your crew is poor quality, subtract 2 from the total. If the crew is good quality, add 2 to the total. If the crew is excellent quality, add 3.

Score 0-4	Calamity; you are killed	turn to **560**
Score 5-9	Crushing defeat; lose 2-12 Stamina	turn to **535**
Score 10-13	Forced to give in; lose 1-6 Stamina	turn to **510**
Score 14-17	The pirates withdraw	turn to **358**
Score 18+	Outright victory	turn to **752**

681

Cross off the codeword *Boysen*.

As darkness approaches, the retreating water uncovers a flat expanse of tidal flats dotted with seaweed-clumped boulders. Crabs run to and fro searching for scraps. Then you see a carriage rumbling in your direction. It is pulled by two huge green horses and seems to have risen straight out of the sea.

The carriage stops and a familiar figure with a flute climbs out. "Ah, you solved my riddle," he says with a smile. "Or is it just luck that brings us both here at this time? Well, it doesn't matter."

He hauls a chest out of the back of the carriage and is about to give it to you when he spots a seashell lying in the wet sand at his feet. Picking it up, he says: "Tell you what—would you rather have what's in the chest, or what's in this shell?"

| Take the chest | turn to **729** |
| Take the shell | turn to **753** |

682

In a hole under an oak tree you find an old **copper pot**. You recall hearing an old folktale in which a man left 50 Shards in such a pot and was rewarded by the fairy folk.

| Leave 50 Shards in the pot | turn to **754** |
| Go on your way | turn to **349** |

683

You help yourself to the pirates' treasure, which amounts to 450 Shards. Record it on your Adventure Sheet. Their hold contains 1 Cargo Unit of grain, which you can add to your own cargo if you have room for it. Your mate advises taking the **pirate captain's head**: "A grisly trophy, perhaps, but often there's a reward if you have proof you've slain such a devil."

You also get a chance to increase in Rank after your stirring leadership in battle. Roll two dice, and if the result is greater than your current Rank you gain a Rank. You also gain 1–6 Stamina points *permanently*; increase your normal (unwounded) Stamina score by the roll of one die. Remember that going up a Rank increases your Defense.

Once you have made the necessary adjustments to your Adventure Sheet, turn to **198**.

684

The sailors clap their hands and roar with approval as the comely mermaid strikes elegant poses in the water. She does not realize they are just trying to lull her natural wariness until you and the mate can cast a net.

Suddenly you act. Wide-eyed, she watches the net hurtle above her through the air. Her mouth distorts into a horrified expression of surprise as she tries to veer away. To catch her you must roll one die and score less than or equal to your Rank—if you roll higher than your Rank, the net missed her.

| Catch her in the net | turn to **732** |
| She gets away | turn to **756** |

685

Without warning, you lunge at the baroness's throat. Her nearest sentries dash forward to grab you, but they may already be too late. Make a COMBAT roll at a Difficulty of 16. If successful, you managed to snap Vanna's neck before the sentries could stop you. A failed COMBAT roll means they drag you off before you can complete the deed.

Either way, your life is forfeit. Sir Debrumas draws his knife and plunges it into your heart. Your head will adorn the spiked gateway outside the castle, as a warning to all would-be assassins, and Estragon the wizard will see to it that you are never restored to life.

686

If you have the codeword *Bisect*, turn to **710**. If not, turn to **734**.

687

You pick up a man who you find clinging to a broken bowsprit. He tells you his vessel was wrecked in a storm. "It seems I alone survived to tell the tale," he says as he tucks into the food you set out for him in your cabin.

Roll two dice:

Score 2-5	turn to **711**
Score 6-8	turn to **735**
Score 9-12	turn to **759**

688

A group of Mannekyn People flit down from the crags to speak with you. They look like monkeys with mauve velvety fur and bat-like wings. They ask if you know one of their species by the name of Tekshin. "He left us to make a living in the land of men, after losing his wings to Pogreta the witch in a foolish gambling game."

Get the codeword *Bullseye* and turn to **640**.

689

You are in a vast chamber. It is dark and hazy with blue resinous smoke. Glimmering lamps sparkle along the distant walls. Ravens flutter among the high black rafters.

Trestles line the room. Seated there are countless people with white faces and red rheumy eyes. Something draws your eyes to the far end of the hall, where a cowled figure sits on a gnarled wooden throne.

Sit at a trestle	turn to **723**
Approach the cowled figure	turn to **747**
Try to leave	turn to **771**

690

The sky is filled with gray scudding clouds, racing ahead of the wind like ghostly galleons in full sail.

Go north	turn to **496**
Go south	turn to **521**
Go east	turn to **446**
Go west	turn to **546**

691

"Confess your sins," says the pardoner you meet along the road. "For a small fee I can grant you absolution."

"How small?"
"Seven Shards."

Pay his fee	turn to **715**
Pass on by	turn to **11**

692

Gradually you begin to see distinct silvery figures wavering in the air in front of you. "We are the spirits of the waterfall," they whisper to you. "We can show you great treasure, but only once."

"One great treasure is enough," you reply glibly.

"You misunderstand. It is not easy to get the treasure. There are snares and challenges. You will have only one chance. If you have not seen and decoded the plaque, you can only rely on luck."

Enigmatic. What will you decide?

Tell them to show you the treasure	turn to **648**
Leave	turn to **716**

693

You are surprised to meet a herald in the livery of the High King of Old Harkuna. "Surely the throne is vacant?" you say. "The barons have now divided the old kingdom among themselves."

The herald nods. "This is true. But my father's father served the last High King, and I have sworn to continue the family tradition."

You watch him ride off. His cause is futile but honorable. Turn to **310**.

694

There is talk of a valuable gem that has recently arrived on a ship from Uttaku.

Steal the gem	turn to **618**
Let it pass	turn to **48**

695

The innkeeper charges an exorbitant 3 Shards a day for board and lodging. Each day you spend here, you can recover 1 Stamina point if injured, up to the limit of your normal unwounded Stamina score. When you are ready to leave, turn to **81**.

696

You enter the cave and edge forward through the gloom. After a while you hear a thundering noise. It is coming from further down the tunnel.

Suddenly a torrent of water comes rushing forward to engulf you. Lose 2–12 Stamina points (the roll of two dice) and, if you survive, turn to **689**.

697

The bull catches you on its horns and tosses you over the hedge, where you land in a pile of manure. A group of nearby peasants find this hilarious. Lose 1–6 Stamina points and all your dignity. Also lose 1 point off your COMBAT score because of the damage to your confidence. Then turn to **199**.

698

Looting the wight's burial mound, you discover treasure worth 200–1200 Shards (roll two dice and multiply by 100). Add this to the cash on your Adventure Sheet and then turn to **222**.

699

You thrust the **peacock feather** over your shoulder, tickling the fiend's nose so that it sneezes violently. As you feel its grip loosen, you break free and run for all you're worth until you are safely away from Castle Orlock. Turn to **268**.

700

There is nothing to guide your choice. You will have to rely on luck. Selecting a door at random, you point to it.

Again the gem in the snake's head gives a flicker of magical light and four of the other doors slowly open, each revealing a poison-tipped dart that would have slain you if you had chosen that door. *Now only two doors remain unopened*, says the snake. *Do you wish to hold to your original choice? I'll give you a last chance to change your mind.*

Stick with your first choice	turn to **724**
Choose the other closed door instead	turn to **748**

701

It is late afternoon when you cross a bridge near a millpond. The seven fools are wading around at the water's edge with rakes in their hands, lunging at the pond. They seem quite agitated, and when you ask what the matter is, one replies: "Just look! The moon's gone and fallen into the pond, and we better have her out by nightfall or who knows what trouble there'll be."

You explain it is just the reflection of the moon, which is palely visible in the sky by this hour. The fools are so relieved that one of them presents you with a **four-leaf clover**. Note it on your Adventure Sheet and then turn to **265**.

702

Two brigands leap out from hiding and menace you with their swords. One is behind you, one in front. "Give it up," they advise. "Money's not worth getting killed over."

Fight them	turn to **726**
Run off	turn to **750**
Hand over your cash	turn to **384**

703

You are given a bed beside the hearth in the common room. There are no other guests. "We don't get many travelers in these parts," explains the innkeeper as he bids you good night.

In the middle of the night you hear a knock on the door. A voice calls from outside: "Is anyone awake? Let me in."

Open the door	turn to **775**
Go back to sleep	turn to **385**

704

A stranger in gray robes sits on the steps of a horse-drawn carriage playing a bulbous flute. As you approach, he looks up and smiles. His teeth gleam white in the beams from the rising moon. He says:

"Read me this riddle and read it aright:
Where shall I next from my carriage alight?
It's east of the sunset, west of the moon,
North of the sea, o'erlooked by a dune.
Such is the spot where we'll make our tryst—
But be prompt, for sometimes it doesn't exist."

Get the codeword *Boysen*. If you have the codewords *Bastion* or *Brush*, cross them off.

The pipeman starts to get back up into his carriage. Pausing, he turns and gives you a wink. "Mind you go straight there,"

he says. "I can't abide being kept waiting."

The horses need no touch of whip to stir them, nor reins to guide them. As soon as the door of the carriage closes, they are off. Turn to **222**.

705

You are on a stretch of windswept shoreline. There is nowhere to go but up the path to the clifftop. Turn to **373**.

706

In a hole under an oak tree you find an old **copper pot**, which you can take if you wish. Then turn to **349**.

707

Instead of sails, the wizards' ship is propelled by a peculiar web of thin copper wires that produces a subsonic hum. You see the three wizards who command the ship standing in the prow, above a figurehead shaped like the snout of a saber-spined dragon. Their long robes of blue and violet silk are decorated with patterns of silver filigree.

Attack the wizards	turn to **731**
Go alongside and hail them	turn to **755**
Sail on	turn to **335**

708

The mermaid seems quite taken with you. Coming right up to the side of the ship, she reaches out of the water and beckons you to lean over to her. Your sailors give a cheer as she takes a mother-of-pearl comb from her hair and touches you with it before shyly diving down out of sight.

"That's a good omen, Captain," affirms the cabin boy. "The touch of a mermaid's comb gives protection from plague."

Note on your Adventure Sheet that you now have Immunity from Disease and Poison. This blessing will work *once* to allow you to ignore the effect of disease or poison.

Now turn to **335**.

709

To qualify for a favor you must either have the title *Paladin of Ravayne* or succeed at a CHARISMA roll at a Difficulty of 16.

Request granted	turn to **591**
Request refused	turn to **342**

710 ❏

If the box here is not checkmarked, put a mark in it now and then turn to **758**. If it is marked already, turn to **734**.

711

The shipwrecked mariner is suffering from a curse that now affects your ship too. Turn to **484**.

712

East of here, the mountains become a sheer column of rock reaching up to the edge of heaven. Westward stretches the Spine of Harkun, said to be the vestiges of a fallen god of ancient times.

Go west	turn to **282**
Go east	*The Plains of Howling Darkness* **300**
Go south	turn to **372**
Go north	*The Plains of Howling Darkness* **200**

713

You can get lodging here for 1 Shard a day. Each day you spend here allows you to recover 1 Stamina point if injured. (Remember that your Stamina cannot go higher than its normal unwounded score.) When you are ready to leave, turn to **191**.

714

Low hills spread across the horizon in all directions. The incessant breeze makes the heather sway like a living thing, but you sense you are alone here on the heath.

Go north	turn to **738**
Go south	turn to **496**
Go east	turn to **521**
Go west	turn to **546**

715

Remember to cross off the 7 Shards. The pardoner gives you a special blessing. This allows you to re-roll any failed SANCTITY roll *once*. After making a second attempt at the roll, whether successful or not, the blessing is used up.

Write SANCTITY *re-roll (one use)* under the blessings on your Adventure Sheet. Then turn to **11**.

716

You are on the banks of the Rainbow River where it meanders between the Haunted Hills and the dreaded Forest of the Forsaken.

Follow the river south	turn to **237**
Go west	turn to **30**
Go east	turn to **122**
Go up into the Haunted Hills	turn to **305**
Enter the Forest of the Forsaken	turn to **7**

717

You meet the wizard Estragon on a lonely stretch of road at dusk. With his wild stare and streaming silver beard, he looks alarming enough. But then you notice you can see right through him.

"This isn't my real self, just a psychic projection," he says.

"Visit me at Castle Ravayne. I might have a quest for you."

Turn to **310**.

718 ❑

If the box above is empty, put a checkmark in it and turn to **537**. If it was marked already, turn to **562**.

719

You go out into the meadows as soon as the sun rises. Early as you are, the place is already teeming with other prospectors and you are forced to make do with a patch of hard soil that you sift through until late afternoon.

Roll two dice:

Score 2-4 turn to **395**
Score 5-8 turn to **420**
Score 9-12 turn to **445**

720

The tunnel is in darkness. You will need either a lantern or a candle to proceed. If you use a candle, cross it off your Adventure Sheet, as it is only good for one use.

Proceed along tunnel turn to **744**
Do not have lantern/candle turn to **716**

721

You are grabbed and hauled in front of the Piepowder Court: seven ruddy-cheeked farmers in homespun smocks who barely know a half-dozen paragraphs of criminal law between them. Although you protest your innocence, as a stranger in the district, you are convicted of theft. You are fined all your cash (cross it off your Adventure Sheet), given a birching, and then left in the stocks to be pelted with rotten fruit. Turn to **199**.

722

You lead it in a merry chase until dawn when, caught by surprise in the full rays of the rising sun, it gives a mournful howl and dissolves away like mist. Turn to **698**.

723

One of the white-faced company pulls you down onto the bench beside him. A cup of thin black liquor is pressed into your hand. "Drink deep," says a sepulchral voice, "for the grave has few other comforts." Turn to **560**.

724

You open the door and a steel bolt shoots out. Lose 3–18 Stamina points (the total of three dice). Even if you survive, you also have to worry about the poison on the bolt's tip, which will slay you unless you have a blessing of Immunity to Disease and Poison. (If you do have such a blessing, remember

to cross it off your Adventure Sheet now that it is used up.)

If you survive, you stagger to your feet to find the snake and the six doors have vanished. Turn to **93**.

725

You find seven simpletons weeping beside a stream. "Oh woe!" cries one. "Our friend is missing—we think he's drowned."

"You think he's drowned? You don't know for sure?"

"We only noticed him missing when it was time for us to go home. We counted ourselves to check we were all here, but even though seven left this morning, now there are but six." He counts his friends: "One, two, three, four, five, six. You see?"

You point out that he's forgotten to count himself.

"So no one drowned at all!" they say, brightening up. "How can we ever repay you?"

"For what?"

"Why, for saving our poor drowned friend."

You cannot help laughing at their idiocy. This is a story you can dine on for weeks. Roll two dice. If the total is higher than your CHARISMA, increase your CHARISMA score by 1. Then turn to **265**.

726

They have an accomplice in hiding who shoots you with an arrow. Roll one die and subtract your armor's Defense bonus (if you have any armor). The remainder is the number of Stamina points you lose. The third brigand then leaps up to join his comrades. Fight them one after the other:

First Brigand, COMBAT 5, Defense 6, Stamina 4
Second Brigand, COMBAT 4, Defense 5, Stamina 4
Third Brigand, COMBAT 3, Defense 4, Stamina 3
Defeat them turn to **353**
Surrender and beg for mercy turn to **384**

727 ❑

If the box is empty, put a checkmark in it and turn to **751**. If the box was marked already, turn to **385**.

728 ❑

The distant lilt of strange music echoes eerily through the dusk from beyond a thick grove of trees. If the box above is not marked, mark it now and turn to **704**. If it is marked already, turn to **486**.

729

You eagerly throw open the lid. An aroma of salt and tar rises from the chest. Inside is a **pearl breastplate (Defense +6)** and a **coral spear (COMBAT +2)**. Record these on your Adventure Sheet.

Bidding you farewell, the stranger climbs back into his carriage. "Wait," you ask. "Who are you?"

His reply is almost drowned out by the fierce whinny of the horses: "They call me Dom Daniel...."

As the carriage turns and speeds back toward the sea, you hear the lilting music of Dom Daniel's pipe keening on the wind. Turn to **705**.

730

You sneak on to the ship, tiptoe into the captain's cabin while he's sleeping off a rum-soaked evening, and steal the gem. The next day you sell it for 400 Shards. Add this to your money and then turn to **48**.

731

They retaliate by hurling spells to distort the weather. The sky turns to the color of burning pitch. Waves lash the sides of your ship. "Merciful gods!" cries the mate. "This is no natural storm. We've had it, skipper!"

To counter the wizards' spells, you must make a MAGIC roll at a Difficulty of 16.

Successful MAGIC roll	turn to **776**
Failed MAGIC roll	turn to **459**

732

The net is hauled up out of the water and bundled aboard. Despite her slender frame, the mermaid struggles like a frenzied shark, thrashing the deck with her tail and spitting curses in the liquid tongue of the undersea folk.

The mate steps forward and cracks her over the head with a cudgel, laying her out cold. A hasty search yields only a **mermaid's comb** and **coral-red tresses**. Either of these can be sold at any market for 50 Shards.

At the mate's advice, you order the mermaid thrown back into the sea before she can come around and lay a curse on the ship. As she sinks below the waves, you raise the mainsail and resume your voyage without further delay. Turn to **335**.

733

"You wish to serve this noble household?" replies Baroness Vanna. "In what capacity?"

What will you suggest?

Spying on her foes	turn to **757**
A diplomatic mission	turn to **777**
Slaying a monster	turn to **391**
Making a map	turn to **416**
Denounce a traitor	turn to **686**
Pay a cash tribute	turn to **662**

734

Which of Vanna's knights will you accuse of plotting against her? The three who are closest to her would logically have the best opportunity to betray her:

Sir Fontesque	turn to **392**
Sir Parpulax	turn to **417**
Sir Gargin	turn to **442**

735

The man you have rescued turns out to be a wealthy merchant from Metriciens. He writes you out a letter of credit amounting to 300 Shards. Add this sum to the money on your Adventure Sheet. "It is a small price to pay for my life!" declares the man, shaking your hand. Turn to **358**.

736

Get the codeword *Bunting*. Delete the **parchment** from your Adventure Sheet and note that you now possess a **map of the mountains** instead. Once you've done that, turn to **712**.

737

It costs 1 Shard a day to stay at the inn. During the time you spend here, you will recover 1 Stamina point if injured, up to the maximum limit set by your normal unwounded Stamina score.

When you are ready to leave, turn to **217**.

738

You quicken your pace, sensing that something important lies just ahead.

Go north	turn to **496**
Go south	turn to **521**
Go east	turn to **546**
Go west	turn to **762**

739

You can recover 2–12 lost Stamina points (the roll of two dice) if injured. Remember that you cannot have more Stamina points than your normal unwounded score. Now it is time for you to travel on once more. Turn to **74**.

740

The pilgrims are on their way to the Abbey of Lacuna, the goddess of the moon.

If you are an initiate of Lacuna, turn to **655**. If not, you can only bid them a safe journey, turn to **355**.

741

Your shortcut across a seemingly empty field proves to be unwise. You are suddenly charged by a ferocious bull that is

intent on decorating its horns with your lower intestine.

Run for it	turn to **199**
Stand and fight	turn to **649**

742

You get to hear about a spice shipment from Ankon-Konu that is due to arrive in port within a few days. "I got the news from a wizard who's just come from Dweomer," says the merchant who is telling you this.

"How come his ship got here before the one with the spice?"

He gives you a knowing smirk. "I said he's a wizard. He probably flew here on a demon's back!"

If you want to invest in the market on the basis of this information, decide how much you're investing (in multiples of 100 Shards) and then turn to **594**.

If you aren't interested in making an investment, turn to **48**.

743

A vagabond in ragged clothes tells you he has lately returned from the Feathered Lands, which lie far to the south across the ocean. "It is a land of marvels," he declares. "There is a hole right through the world there, and men study the stars through it. Another town is built around the feet of a great colossus that holds up the sky. On the east coast are plains where a tribe of gold-skinned men feud with a tribe who have blue skin. In the deepest desert they keep a flotilla of ships, and in the western jungles I saw clumps of moss crawling like caterpillars."

By comparison, Golnir is quite humdrum. Turn to **246**.

744

The tunnel leads to a chamber deep inside the cliff. Stalactites as fine as silver threads hang from the ceiling, surrounding a table of rock where there are three chests. One is of corroded copper, one of rusty iron, and one of tarnished silver.

Open the copper chest	turn to **768**
Open the iron chest	turn to **402**
Open the silver chest	turn to **427**

745

You underestimated the potency of the local brew. Unless you have a blessing of Immunity to Disease and Poison, you wake up in a ditch with a pounding headache. It is late morning and the fair is packing up. You have lost half your money (cross it off your Adventure Sheet) but have somehow managed to acquire a **candle**, a **silver horseshoe,** and a **peacock's feather**. Turn to **199**.

746

With silent efficiency, the highwaymen divest you of your purse. Cross off all the money on your Adventure Sheet, then turn to **55**.

747

Your footsteps echo hollowly on the polished panels of the floor. The cowled figure peers down at you and says: "Blood and breath, sweat and sinew. Here is one from the land of mortals, who still bears the special stench of life. You did not come here by the usual route, mortal."

If you are an initiate of Tyrnai	turn to **784**
If an initiate of Nagil	turn to **405**
Otherwise	turn to **723**

748

You ease the door open with bated breath, fearing that at any moment something horrible will leap out to confront you. But the snake was as good as its word—or as good as its thought, rather. Beyond the door lies a heap of treasure amounting to 400 Shards. Add this sum to your Adventure Sheet.

There you are, says the snake telepathically. You sense an undercurrent of satisfaction in its mind. Has it tricked you somehow? Is there an even greater treasure beyond the other door?

Open the other closed door as well	turn to **724**
Leave now	turn to **93**

749

It begins to drizzle. Strolling along, you see seven worried shepherds wading about in the middle of a stream waving their crooks in the air. Their dogs are watching in amazement from the bank. "Whatever are you doing?" you ask.

"We've decided to herd fish instead of sheep, because you

can't sell mutton on Friday," replies one.

"But now that it's raining, we're trying to round the fish up so they don't get wet," puts in another.

Shaking your head, you set off down the road. Turn to **265**.

750

A third brigand, who had remained in hiding in case you made a break for it, now leaps up and shoots off an arrow. Roll one die and subtract your armor's Defense bonus (if you have any armor). The remainder is the number of Stamina points you lose.

If you survive, you race off with the three brigands in close pursuit. To shake them off you must make a SCOUTING roll at a Difficulty of 10. If you fail, they'll catch you.

Successful SCOUTING roll	turn to **78**
Failed SCOUTING roll	turn to **384**

751

You are given a nourishing plate of stew with hunks of freshly baked bread, washed down with cool refreshing ale. While you eat, the innkeeper makes you up a bed in the cozy nook beside the hearth.

If you have a blessing of Immunity to Disease and Poison, cross it off and turn to **385**. Otherwise turn to **560**.

752

You help yourself to the pirates' treasure, which amounts to 750 Shards. Record it on your Adventure Sheet. Their ship's hold contains 1 Cargo Unit of minerals, which you can add to your own cargo if you have room for it. Your mate advises taking the **pirate captain's head**: "A grisly trophy, perhaps, but often there's a reward if you have proof you've slain such a devil."

You also get a chance to increase in Rank after your stirring leadership in battle. Roll two dice, and if the result is greater than your current Rank you gain a Rank. You also gain 1–6 Stamina points *permanently;* increase your normal (unwounded) Stamina score by the roll of one die. Remember that going up a Rank increases your Defense.

Once you have made the necessary adjustments to your Adventure Sheet, turn to **358**.

753

The stranger holds the shell to your ear. At first there is nothing to be heard, but then a spectral voice begins to whisper. It tells you many secrets of ancient wisdom.

Gain one Rank. Going up in Rank will increase your Defense, and also gives you an additional 1–6 Stamina points *permanently*—i.e. increase your unwounded Stamina score by the roll of one die.

Bidding you farewell, the stranger climbs back into his carriage. "Wait," you ask. "Who are you?"

His reply is almost drowned out by the fierce whinny of the horses: "They call me Dom Daniel."

As the carriage turns and speeds back toward the sea, you hear the lilting music of Dom Daniel's pipe wailing on the wind. Turn to **705**.

754 ❏

If the box is empty, put a checkmark in it and turn to **619**. If it was already marked, turn to **643**.

755

The wizards say you should apply to one of the sorcerous colleges in Dweomer, but not to bother if you're a priest. "To be godly, a person must close their mind to life's mysteries."

Thanking them for their advice, you sail off. Turn to **335**.

756

The mermaid says something in an unknown language. It is only a single word and, though she only seems to whisper, it resounds across the water like the tolling of a bell. Then, giving you a last look of satisfaction, she dives under the gray pall of the sea.

"That's ruined us," says the mate grimly. "We're cursed now for sure."

Turn to **434**.

757 ❏

If the box above is empty, put a checkmark in it now and turn to **441**. If the box is marked and you have the codeword *Element*, turn to **466**. If the box is marked and you do not have *Element*, turn to **491**.

758

You give proof of treachery on the part of Sir Bredubar, Vanna's own half brother. He screams oaths of vengeance at the top of his lungs and lunges toward you with drawn dagger, but the Baroness' guards haul him away.

"I shall not even execute him," says Vanna. "He does not deserve a clean death. Let him rot in the dungeons."

Get the codeword *Bashful* and turn to **342**.

759

The man was navigator aboard a merchant ship that plied the trading routes between Chambara, Smogmaw, and Metriciens. During the journey he teaches you something of the science of navigation. Roll two dice, and if you get higher than your SCOUTING score, add 1 to it.

Then turn to **358**.

760 ❑

If the box above is empty, put a checkmark in it and turn to **469**. If it is already marked, turn to **172**.

761

The Saucy Goblin Inn has a tariff of 1 Shard a day. During the time you spend here, you will recover 1 Stamina point (if injured) up to the maximum limit set by your normal unwounded Stamina score. When you are ready to leave, turn to **242**.

762 ❑

If the box is empty, put a checkmark in it and turn to **471**. If it is marked already, turn to **496**.

763

You spend weeks in meditation and study. Roll one die. If the number rolled is higher than your MAGIC score, increase it by 1.

"Books alone are not enough. You must also study the secret patterns of nature," says the monk in charge of the scriptorium.

Taking this advice to heart, you set out again on your travels. Turn to **74**.

764

It is the first time you have seen an entire village reduced to panic because of one bent-backed old woman. "Can't you see the marks of plague on her face?" screeches one man, his face contorted in hate. "She must be cast out!"

"Please...." wheezes the old woman. "I only want a cup of water, then I'll be on my way."

Give her the water	turn to **453**
Ignore the incident	turn to **355**

765

You cannot resist the temptation to stop off at the fair. Two whole fields are covered with gaudily colored tents and stalls where you can watch juggling, acrobatics, dancing bears, and singing birds. Roll two dice:

Score 2-4	Taken for a thief	turn to **721**
Score 5-7	Get drunk on nettle beer	turn to **745**
Score 8-12	Win a prize	turn to **769**

766

You hear a tale of a merchant who resolved to do business with the trau, the eldritch race that dwells in caverns below the world. Unfortunately the merchant did not foresee that the trau have no use for human coinage. They bundled him up and took him off to their subterranean lairs.

"What did they do with him?" you ask the man who is telling the story.

He's not sure. "Boiled him down to make oil for their lamps, I expect."

Turn to **48**.

767

A troll emerges from behind a rock, casting his net to entangle you. His three heads converse on the topic of how you should be cooked:

"Boiled!" declares the head with lurid red eyes.

"Pah! Stewed," asserts the head with tusks.

"Roasted, surely?" suggests the smallest head.

Join in the discussion	turn to **575**
Try to free yourself	turn to **647**

768

Inside you find a sword and a shield. A voice at your shoulder makes you jump in alarm, but it is only one of the spirits that has followed you down the tunnel. "You must choose one of these items," it says.

Take the sword	turn to **452**
Take the shield	turn to **477**

769

You line up at a coconut throw, only instead of coconuts the cups contain human heads. When you point out to the stall-holder that this is a rather grisly joke, he can only shrug. "I am a worshipper of the god Nagil, and dead things do not revolt me in the least. Anyhow, look along the line. There are plenty of people willing to throw a few balls if you're not."

You throw three balls and manage to win a **pirate captain's head**. Note it on your Adventure Sheet and turn to **199**.

770

They say nothing in response to your defiance, but you sense they are almost pleased to have the opportunity to fight you. Do battle with each in turn:

1st Highwayman, COMBAT 5, Defense 7, Stamina 7
2nd Highwayman, COMBAT 5, Defense 7, Stamina 7
3rd Highwayman, COMBAT 4, Defense 5, Stamina 4

If you flee, you will get shot in the back with the crossbow that the third man is carrying; roll two dice and subtract your armor's Defense bonus to find out how many Stamina points of damage it does.

Flee	turn to **55**
Win	turn to **404**

771

You stumble through the haze toward double doors of black wood with huge copper rivets. They look like the doors of a tomb. A tomb seen from the inside. To open the doors and escape, you must make a MAGIC roll at a Difficulty of 15.

Successful MAGIC roll	turn to **99**
Failed MAGIC roll	turn to **723**

772

"Turn back," warns a voice from nowhere. "It isn't safe to stray down this path."

You look around, but can see no one. Perhaps the voice was only a trick of your overwrought imagination?

Turn back	turn to **22**
Continue along the path	turn to **382**

773

You pass a poor old tramp who has no pants. "I hung them on a branch yesterday while I saw to a call of nature," he says. "But some rascal made off with them."

The following morning you see seven fools watering a tree by the side of the road. "It's a clothing tree," they explain. "We got some pants off it a couple of days ago, and now we're watering it to see if we can get a coat and hat as well."

"You preposterous oafs," is all you can say.

As you continue along the road, you hear one of them say: "Hey, aren't we supposed to fill the watering can first?"

Turn to **265**.

774

He takes his leave of you the next day, saying that he must make his way back toward the river to meet a friend. An hour after he has gone, you become suspicious. Checking your money pouch, you discover that he has stolen all your cash. Cross it off your Adventure Sheet and turn to **349**.

775

Throwing open the door, you shiver as a gust of wind blows cold drizzle in your face. "Well, hurry up and enter, then!" you call out irritably.

"Thank you," says a tall gentleman in a cloak. He sweeps past you into the room, showing a smile with rather too many sharp white teeth, and waits for you to close the door.

You have a nasty feeling about this. You cannot reach your belongings (including armor and weapons) because the stranger is standing between you and the hearth.

Run out into the night	turn to **387**
Go back to bed	turn to **412**

776

The three wizards scowl to see you dispel their enchantment so easily. Now it is your turn. You evoke a potent curse that they are hard-pressed to resist. Make a MAGIC roll at a Difficulty of 17.

Successful MAGIC roll	turn to **389**
Failed MAGIC roll	turn to **414**

777 ❏

If the box above is empty, put a checkmark in it now and turn to **516**. If the box is marked and you have a **diplomatic letter**, turn to **541**. If the box is marked and you do not have a **diplomatic letter**, turn to **491**.

778

The tavern costs you 1 Shard a day. Each day you spend here, you can recover 1 Stamina point if injured, up to the limit of your normal unwounded Stamina score. When you are ready to leave, turn to **48**.

779

The market at Haggart's Corner amounts to just a few shops whose dusty shelves suggest they don't do a roaring trade. "People prefer to do business with the trau," says one store-keeper with a shrug. "Who can compete?"

Perhaps you will find a bargain here all the same:

Armor	To buy	To sell
Leather (Defense +1)	50 Shards	45 Shards
Ring mail (Defense +2)	100 Shards	90 Shards

Weapons (sword, axe, etc)	To buy	To sell
Without COMBAT bonus	50 Shards	40 Shards
COMBAT bonus +1	200 Shards	

Magical equipment	To buy	To sell
Amber wand (MAGIC +1)	500 Shards	400 Shards
Ebony wand (MAGIC +2)	—	800 Shards
Cobalt wand (MAGIC +3)	—	1600 Shards

Other items	To buy	To sell
Lockpicks (THIEVERY +1)	300 Shards	270 Shards
Compass (SCOUTING +1)	500 Shards	450 Shards
Rope	—	45 Shards
Candle	1 Shard	1 Shard
Fairy mead	—	150 Shards

Items that have no purchase price listed are not available here. When you've completed your business, turn to **242**.

780

You kneel before the bare stone altar carved in the shape of an anvil. There is no effigy here to represent the god. There is no need for such a thing. Worshippers of Molhern believe his essence can be discerned in all of creation.

Make a SANCTITY roll at a Difficulty of 12.

Successful SANCTITY roll	turn to **397**
Failed SANCTITY roll	turn to **422**

781

Thick black clouds pile up along the horizon. If you have the blessing of Alvir and Valmir, which confers Safety from Storms, you can ignore the storm. Cross off your blessing and turn to *The War-Torn Kingdom* **240**.

Otherwise the storm hits with full fury. Roll one die:

Score 1–3	Ship sinks	turn to **553**
Score 4–6	You weather the storm	*The War-Torn Kingdom* **240**

782

"You've got to wait inside that ring of standing stones," says a flower seller, pointing out across the meadows. "Some nights the trau will come. More often they won't. And mind that you keep one Mithral to pay your toll when leaving the standing stones, or you won't be seen this side of the sky again!"

"What's a Mithral?" says her husband, overhearing the conversation.

She gives him a clout on the ear. "Old fool! If you don't know that, you'd better keep your nose out of trau business."

Go out to the standing stones	turn to **520**
Visit the temple of Lacuna	turn to **294**
Take lodging at an inn	turn to **761**
Leave the town	turn to **173**

783

The stranger says he will prove his holiness by preaching a sermon to the local cats, "since cats are known to be ungodly creatures."

He starts to screech and howl in a most unearthly way, and sure enough after a few minutes a group of assorted cats has collected by the roadside to listen.

"You see?" says the stranger. "They listened raptly, the little darlings. I'm sure they'll go home better cats for that sermon. Now it's your turn...."

Make a SCOUTING roll at a Difficulty of 12.

Successful SCOUTING roll	turn to **403**
Failed SCOUTING roll	turn to **428**

784

"My brother has already claimed you. You cannot stay here," intones the death god. He extends a claw-like hand, and you feel yourself flung away by magic. Turn to **99**.

785

Against the last blood-red swathes of sunset, a vast ship heaves into view. As it gets closer and you are able to get a true impression of its size, awe gradually gives way to fear. It is like a fortress built of oak. Even the tallest pine tree would be dwarfed by its masts, and those black sails are like the canopy of night.

"She's the dread Nagil's flagship," whispers the mate. "Her sailors are not living men."

Go aboard the Ship of Souls	turn to **433**
Sail away	turn to **221**

786

The militiamen seize you. "I can't believe it!" gasps their sergeant in disgust. "What's the world coming to when murderers openly wander about the countryside showing off their handiwork?"

You appeal to the severed head to explain, but it chooses to keep its opinions to itself. The militiamen are now convinced you are mad as well as evil. You will have a hard time convincing them otherwise. Try to make a CHARISMA roll at a Difficulty of 16.

Successful CHARISMA roll	turn to **483**
Failed CHARISMA roll	turn to **458**

Adventurer's Journal

For the keeping of notes

Adventurer's Journal

For the keeping of notes

Adventurer's Journal

For the keeping of notes

Adventure Sheet

NAME

PROFESSION

GOD

RANK

DEFENSE

ABILITY   **SCORE**

CHARISMA	
COMBAT	
MAGIC	
SANCTITY	
SCOUTING	
THIEVERY	

POSSESSIONS (maximum of 12)

STAMINA

When unwounded	
Current	

RESURRECTION ARRANGEMENTS

MONEY

TITLES AND HONORS

BLESSINGS

Adventure Sheet

NAME

PROFESSION

GOD

RANK

DEFENSE

ABILITY   **SCORE**

CHARISMA

COMBAT

MAGIC

SANCTITY

SCOUTING

THIEVERY

POSSESSIONS (maximum of 12)

STAMINA

When unwounded

Current

RESURRECTION ARRANGEMENTS

MONEY

TITLES AND HONORS

BLESSINGS

Adventure Sheet

NAME

PROFESSION

GOD

RANK

DEFENSE

ABILITY
SCORE

CHARISMA

COMBAT

MAGIC

SANCTITY

SCOUTING

THIEVERY

POSSESSIONS (maximum of 12)

STAMINA

When unwounded

Current

RESURRECTION ARRANGEMENTS

MONEY

TITLES AND HONORS

BLESSINGS

Adventure Sheet

NAME

PROFESSION

GOD

RANK

DEFENSE

ABILITY   **SCORE**

CHARISMA

COMBAT

MAGIC

SANCTITY

SCOUTING

THIEVERY

POSSESSIONS (maximum of 12)

STAMINA

When unwounded

Current

RESURRECTION ARRANGEMENTS

MONEY

TITLES AND HONORS

BLESSINGS

Adventure Sheet

NAME

PROFESSION

GOD

RANK

DEFENSE

ABILITY   **SCORE**

CHARISMA

COMBAT

MAGIC

SANCTITY

SCOUTING

THIEVERY

STAMINA

When unwounded

Current

POSSESSIONS (maximum of 12)

RESURRECTION ARRANGEMENTS

MONEY

TITLES AND HONORS

BLESSINGS

 # Adventure Sheet

NAME

PROFESSION

GOD

RANK

DEFENSE

ABILITY   **SCORE**

CHARISMA

COMBAT

MAGIC

SANCTITY

SCOUTING

THIEVERY

POSSESSIONS (maximum of 12)

STAMINA

When unwounded

Current

RESURRECTION ARRANGEMENTS

MONEY

TITLES AND HONORS

BLESSINGS

Adventure Sheet

NAME

PROFESSION

GOD

RANK

DEFENSE

ABILITY   **SCORE**

CHARISMA	
COMBAT	
MAGIC	
SANCTITY	
SCOUTING	
THIEVERY	

POSSESSIONS (maximum of 12)

STAMINA

| When unwounded | |
| Current | |

RESURRECTION ARRANGEMENTS

MONEY

TITLES AND HONORS

BLESSINGS

Adventure Sheet

NAME

PROFESSION

GOD

RANK

DEFENSE

ABILITY   **SCORE**

CHARISMA

COMBAT

MAGIC

SANCTITY

SCOUTING

THIEVERY

STAMINA

When unwounded

Current

RESURRECTION ARRANGEMENTS

TITLES AND HONORS

POSSESSIONS (maximum of 12)

MONEY

BLESSINGS

Adventure Sheet

NAME

PROFESSION

GOD

RANK

DEFENSE

ABILITY   **SCORE**

CHARISMA

COMBAT

MAGIC

SANCTITY

SCOUTING

THIEVERY

STAMINA

When unwounded

Current

RESURRECTION ARRANGEMENTS

TITLES AND HONORS

POSSESSIONS (maximum of 12)

MONEY

BLESSINGS

Adventure Sheet

NAME

PROFESSION

GOD

RANK

DEFENSE

ABILITY   **SCORE**

CHARISMA

COMBAT

MAGIC

SANCTITY

SCOUTING

THIEVERY

POSSESSIONS (maximum of 12)

STAMINA

When unwounded

Current

RESURRECTION ARRANGEMENTS

MONEY

TITLES AND HONORS

BLESSINGS

Adventure Sheet

NAME

PROFESSION

GOD

RANK

DEFENSE

ABILITY   **SCORE**

CHARISMA

COMBAT

MAGIC

SANCTITY

SCOUTING

THIEVERY

POSSESSIONS (maximum of 12)

STAMINA

When unwounded

Current

RESURRECTION ARRANGEMENTS

MONEY

TITLES AND HONORS

BLESSINGS

CODEWORDS

☐ Bait	☐ Bookworm
☐ Baluster	☐ Bosky
☐ Barnacle	☐ Bounty
☐ Bashful	☐ Boysen
☐ Bastion	☐ Bridoon
☐ Beach	☐ Brisket
☐ Beltane	☐ Brush
☐ Bilge	☐ Bullion
☐ Bisect	☐ Bullseye
☐ Blemish	☐ Bumble
☐ Bobbin	☐ Bunting
☐ Bones	☐ Buzz

QUICK RULES

To use an ability (COMBAT, THIEVERY, and so on), roll two dice and add your score in the ability. To succeed you must roll higher than the Difficulty of the task.

Example:
You want to calm down an angry innkeeper. This requires a CHARISMA roll at a Difficulty of 10. Say you have a CHARISMA score of 6. This means that you would have to get 5 or more on two dice to succeed.

Fighting involves a series of COMBAT rolls. The Difficulty of the roll is equal to the opponent's Defense score. (Your Defense is equal to your Rank PLUS your armor bonus PLUS your COMBAT score.) The amount you beat the Difficulty by is the number of Stamina points that your opponent loses.

That's pretty much all you need to know. If you have any detailed queries, consult the rules section on pages 5–7.

SHIP'S MANIFEST

Ship type	Name	Crew quality	Cargo capacity	Current cargo	Where docked